Front Porch
Stories

D1606521

Nancy R. Ward

ISBN 978-1-64559-632-5 (Paperback)
ISBN 978-1-64559-633-2 (Digital)

Copyright © 2019 Nancy R. Ward
All rights reserved
First Edition

All rights reserved. No part of this publication may be reproduced, distributed, or transmitted in any form or by any means, including photocopying, recording, or other electronic or mechanical methods without the prior written permission of the publisher. For permission requests, solicit the publisher via the address below.

Covenant Books, Inc.
11661 Hwy 707
Murrells Inlet, SC 29576
www.covenantbooks.com

This book is dedicated to my daughter,
Lori; son-in-law, Lee; my son, Alan and my
granddaughters, Cecelia and Charlotte. I love
you more than words could ever express.

Also to Ellen; Anita and Frank; and Jim and Cheryl.

Acknowledgment

I would like to say a very special thank you to the best co-workers and friends I could ever ask for. They have been a support group that I will forever cherish. These people listened, read, shared their thoughts and most of all, encouraged me to make this dream come true.

I could not have done this without each of you.

Contents

Bless Your Heart, Sir..11

The Adventure to Matthew's Island.......................31

Rick's Place...53

Changed Lives...73

Loral Lake Inn...113

Home for the Holidays at Loral Lake Inn............139

Town Picnic at Loral Lake...................................159

Bless Your Heart, Sir

I remember as a young girl, spending our family vacations at North Myrtle Beach. We always stayed at the beach house that our daddy and other firemen from our small town built. They wanted their families to have a place to go and enjoy during the summer months. We always seemed to be at the same spot on the strand during the day. It was our place at the beach.

One night during the week, our parents would take us out to eat a seafood meal. We would go to Calabash, where every restaurant on Calabash Row was crowded. People from all over the country would be there to get fish, shrimp, oysters, crab, and all of the fixings to go with it. And believe me when I say that the food was worth the wait because sometimes we had to stand in long lines just to be seated. We thought that was part of the experience and part of the fun of a week at the beach.

Another night during the week, our parents would take us to the Pavilion. We would ride the rides, play the games, eat cotton candy and candied apples, and we would jump on the trampolines. Of course, no vacation would have ever been complete without our family game of carpet golf. The place was always crowded but never once did our parents worry about us getting lost or separated from them.

Going to the beach one week each year was something that was part of who we were.

As we got older, my sisters married and my brother moved away. No matter where we were, we always found a way to come back for our family vacation.

When I was in my early twenties, we went to the beach for our annual trip. The first day, after everyone had come in for the day and supper had been finished and the dishes washed and put away, I decided to walk back down to the beach with a blanket and the book I was reading to have some time to myself. As I spread my blanket out and settled down to read, I realized I was alone on the beach. It was not long before another couple came out of the motel behind where I was sitting. The man was carrying their chairs and towels. The lady had a small cooler. For some reason, they caught my attention, and I sat and watched them for a few minutes. I am not sure why, but it seemed interesting to me that the woman looked to be a good bit older than the man. As they approached the area where I was, I politely nodded and said hello. I told them that I hoped they were enjoying the beach.

After getting their things in place, they ran into the water holding hands and laughing. It seemed strange to see a couple acting like young teenagers in love. I watched as they played. I could not help but think of how it must feel to have someone make another person that happy. I watched them for a while and felt such a calm joy knowing that people could be happy together no matter the circumstances and no matter the age.

After a few minutes, I went back to reading my book. I did not pay any attention to anyone else on the beach. I was so involved in reading that I seemed to block the rest of the world out. This was my time to relax. Occasionally I would look up and see them still playing in the water.

Some time had passed, and the sun was beginning to go down. It was time to pack up and head back to the house. As I started packing, I noticed the man coming toward me. He was by himself.

"Hi, sir, I noticed the two of you out in the water." I commented, "It was good to see a couple having that much fun playing around like that. You looked like children playing. Is she still with you?"

He replied in a kind, gentle voice, "No, she decided to go back up to the room, and I came over to gather up our things. She was tired and wanted to rest. It was fun out there. I have not done that in quite a long time. What about you? Are you from around here?"

I answered, "We live about an hour away, so we get to come to the beach every year. North Myrtle Beach is like a second home to us. How about y'all? Have you been here before?"

"No, this is my first time here. I have traveled all up and down the East Coast, but this is the first time I have visited the Myrtle Beach area. My friend has been here before so that's why we came."

"Well, I hope the two of you enjoy our Southern hospitality and have a wonderful week."

I never thought twice about speaking to him. That was just what you did in South Carolina. During those years, it just seemed to be a way of welcoming people to the coast of South Carolina. He gathered his things, gave me a smile, and walked on up to the motel.

After getting back to the house and taking a shower, it was time to sit back and watch television with my family. The television was on, and just as usual, there was a game of rummy going on with my dad and a couple of other family members. Our week at the beach had begun.

"Mama, I watched a couple on the beach today. They seemed so happy. I don't know why, but I could not help but notice that the lady was older than the man. They seemed to be having the best time playing in the water together. I wish I had that type of love in my life."

Mama said in only the way she could, "Honey, one day you will. God has just the right person out there for you, and when the time is right, He will send him to you. Just be patient. All in His timing. All in His good timing. As for now, just be thankful that the couple on the beach has found their happiness."

I replied, "They were jumping the waves. He was holding her and letting the waves hit him instead of her. You know, I have never seen the beach as quiet as it was tonight. There weren't people walking up and down the beach. Children weren't out playing. It was very quiet. It was just that couple and me as far as I could see."

Mama responded, "It could be that the heat has everyone enjoying the inside since most people have air conditioners now. Can you remember the weeks we had here when you were young and there was no air conditioning? Now we seem to be spoiled and staying inside on these July days is a little more inviting than running around in the hot sun."

"Yes, and *do* you remember that one strange week that Daddy had to turn the heat on? I never thought it could be cold in South Carolina during July."

"I do remember," Mama said. "That week was not a week to see people playing in the water. We all stayed out of the water and near the heater since I had only packed summer clothes."

As we sat and talked about things going on in our lives, there was a news break. By this time, everyone else had gone to bed so it was just my mother and me watching. The story was about a woman whose body had washed up on the beach about five miles from where we were staying. The lady did not have any identification on her, but she fit the description of the woman I had been watching earlier. She appeared to be in her late fifties or early sixties and weighed about two hundred pounds.

I stared at the television, waiting to hear what he would say next. That is when they showed her picture I could not believe it. The news said she had been strangled and left in the water. Her body had floated down the beach and washed up on shore. People taking a late-night walk had seen the body and called the police. The police were asking anyone with information to please contact them.

"Mama, what should I do? Should I tell them that I think I saw her with a man? Should I tell them that he had spoken to me as he walked back to his motel? Should I stay quiet? Do you think he will remember me? Will he recognize me from the beach if I see him again? What should I do?"

"First things first, you need to calm down, and I will go get your daddy. Just calm down."

We woke Daddy, and the three of us talked about what we should do. We decided that my mother and I would drive to the police station early the next morning and at least tell them that I thought I had seen someone that looked like the lady on the news break. I would tell that she and a man were together on the beach. I would tell them the name of the motel, and I would give them a description of the man. This may not be the same person, but it was the right thing to do. Yes, this was the right thing to do.

Needless to say, it was a long night with very little sleep. We got to the police station early the next morning.

"Sir, I am here about the newsbreak we saw on television last night. Is there someone I can talk with? I think I may have seen the lady who died. She was on the beach with a man. They were in front of the Ocean Drive Motel at about seven in the evening. They were playing in the water, but then he came back up to get their stuff by himself. He said his friend had already gone back up to the motel."

The policeman asked, "Can you describe him?"

"He looked like he was in his early forties with dark hair and bright blue eyes. He had a mark on his left shoulder. It was small but looked like a tattoo of a bird. I am really not quite sure about that though."

The policeman continued. "Did you speak to them at all?"

"I spoke to them when they put their stuff down and to him when he gathered it all back up. He seemed polite," I answered.

"Is there anything else that you can remember about either of them?" he asked.

"Not really," I answered. "I was reading and did not pay much attention to them."

"If you remember anything else, please be sure to let us know." As we walked out, the policeman called out to me, "Miss, please be very careful. We will let you know if we find out anything about them. Just keep your guard up. We appreciate you coming in and giving us this information."

"Thank you, officer, we will," I replied.

That day, we went back down to the beach. My family and I watched carefully to see if he was there. We did not see him all day. I thought that he had probably left and had gotten as far away as he could. I was sure he would not stay around. So once again after supper, I walked back down to the beach with my blanket and book and continued reading. But this time I did not feel the calm, peaceful feeling that being on the beach always gave me. I felt very uncomfortable. I felt as if I was being watched and as if someone was very close by.

For the rest of the week, I tried to let those feelings go, but they kept getting stronger. Everywhere we went and everything I did, I felt as if I was being watched. I tried to talk to my family about it, and everyone just felt that it was because of what I thought I had seen. We had no proof that this man was involved in any way.

For the next few days, my routine stayed pretty much the same. Each day that I went to the beach, I felt as if someone was near me. Each day I felt like someone was following me and watching everything I did.

The tradition of going out to supper continued. We drove to Calabash and ate a fantastic seafood dinner. I remember thinking that even if someone was following us, he would not say anything to me in a crowded place. I tried very hard to relax. I kept looking around to make sure nobody was watching us. That is when I noticed my daddy was doing the same thing. Even though he was telling me I was being silly to think I was being followed, I think he was thinking the same thing. He just looked at me and smiled and never said a word about it.

After the fourth day, I was convinced that I was being followed, and I was beginning to get even more nervous. There was a knock at the door. It was the police officer who had spoken to me at the police station.

"Miss, we just wanted to check on you and see if you had seen the man from the other night anymore," the police officer said with concern in his voice.

"No, sir. I have looked every time we have gone back to the beach. I have not seen him. I was hoping that he was gone and would never come back. But I do feel like someone is watching me or following me. Wherever we go, I feel like there is someone looking at me. My parents think I am imagining it, but it feels too real not to be true."

The officer asked, "Would you take a look at a picture and tell us if it is the same man?"

"Yes, sir. I am not sure if I will recognize him though. Do you know who he is?"

"If it is the man in the picture, he is from Virginia. His name is Stanley Stevens. He has a pattern of traveling around and finding older women to get involved with, and then he takes their money."

As he showed me the picture, I realized it was the same man. He had the same smile that I had seen when he spoke to me. They thanked me and left without saying much else.

For the rest of the week, each day seemed to be the same. I would go down to the beach during the day and sit out in the Sun with my family. We would go back up to the house in the afternoon and fix supper and sit at the table and talk about our day. After supper, we would clean the dishes. I would always go back down to the beach and sit on my blanket and read my book. Nobody seemed to be around.

On our last night there, I went back down to the beach for one last time. I looked up to see a man walking toward me. I noticed that it was the man I had seen with the lady. What should I do? Should I run? Should I play dumb and act as if I did not know anything? Should I say anything to him? Oh no, what should I do? Then I thought that I had this. After all, I was a Southern lady who had been born and raised in South Carolina. I could handle this without any problems—or so I tried to convince myself as he got closer.

He approached me with a smile and spoke as if we had known each other all our lives. "Well, hello. It is good to see that you are still here. It certainly has been hot this week. Have you enjoyed your stay?"

"Yes, sir. It has been a very quiet, uneventful week," I said, trying to sound convincing.

"I noticed you are still reading. Is it the same book you had the other night? You must really enjoy reading."

"I do. When I start reading, I can hardly put the book down. It's as if everything else around me is gone, and it is just me and my book. Have you and your friend enjoyed your stay in our great state?"

"I have. I have visited Charleston and the Isle of Palm and even walked around the Pavilion one night. My lady friend decided to go back home. She had some things she needed to take care of. She left the other day, but I decided not to let that stop me from enjoying my trip."

By this time, I was feeling scared. I thought the thing to do was to find a way to just walk away. "My family is expecting me back, so I should leave. I am glad that you have enjoyed your week. You should come back again sometime. As they say, 'smiling faces, beautiful places' is what South Carolina is all about."

I quickly gathered my things together and started to head back to the house. He grabbed my arm and led me down the beach. I told him to let me go or I would scream. Unfortunately there did not seem to be anyone around to hear me scream. I screamed over and over again, but nobody seemed to hear.

"You need to let me go. I do not want to go with you. I mean it, let me go. My family is waiting for me. You are hurting me. Let me go."

"Not this time. You and I both know that you saw me on the beach with Alana. You may have been reading your book, but I saw you watching us. I know you saw me with her. Don't act so surprised."

"Yes, I did. You two were having a good time. What has that got to do with me? Why should I care if you were on the beach with someone or not? Who are you? Why are you trying to hurt me?"

As we continued down the beach, someone caught my eye. A man was walking near the motels and houses but not in clear site of the beach. He motioned to me. I first thought he was going to help the other man kill me. Then I realized there were several other people all watching from different places. I thought that was my chance. I had to pull away from this man and run toward the motels. I had to get away.

"Just let me go. I have not done anything to you. You can't do this. Let me go. Let me go *now*!"

Just then I pushed back as hard as I could, and he tripped in the sand. I ran as fast as I could toward the motel where the other people were. Several people came out from what seemed to be nowhere and ran toward us. They surrounded the man as he was trying to get up. One of the men grabbed him. Another man grabbed my arm and told me to stop running. He told me they were the police.

"You are okay now. We have you. You are safe. Just calm down and let me get your family for you. We are the ones that have been watching you and staying close to you all week. We were watching for this monster to show back up."

The police officer called my parents, and they met us at the police station. We were put into a room where they asked me many questions, and I was given a chance to tell the officers what had just happened between me and the man from the beach.

The police explained to my parents and me that they had been watching me all week. The police knew who this man was, and they also knew he would try to find me. He had done this before and had been on the run for years. They knew that his pattern was to watch for women alone on the beach and try to befriend them. He would then convince them that he loved them, and he would take every penny they had and then leave them alone and broke. Unfortunately in two other cases, the women had also been found dead. When I identified the picture, they knew this was their chance to get him. If they had told me, I would not be able to stay calm, and he would get away. If he realized I knew what was going on, he would be more likely to harm me. So they had stayed close by and had watched me very closely.

I knew that he was in the same police station and that he knew that I was there. I was told that I could leave. My parents and I were standing in the hall, talking to the police officer. Another officer was taking him to a holding area of the police station. They walked right past us.

"I will be back after you. I will be back."

I smiled at him and said, "Bless your heart, sir. I hope you do come back to South Carolina and do be sure to come by and visit my family. I am quite sure it will be a visit that you will never forget."

Our family went back home to our small town and our regular day-to-day routines. We tried to put this vacation behind us and tried not to think about him.

In the next few months, Stanley Stevens was put on trial for murder. He would be tried in South Carolina for this murder and then would be taken to Virginia for the other two. He would be charged with stealing money from a number of women and with the attempted kidnapping of me. People who had lived to tell the story of what he had done to them were there to testify against him. One lady after another told the story of how he pretended to love her and then stole everything she had. Each one shared a sense of shame and sadness that they allowed themselves to be fooled by him. Each one of these ladies played a big role in ending his string of crimes. And through testifying, they seemed to find a sense of peace.

I was also called to testify. I told of the night I first saw them and how it looked as if they were just a happy couple playing around in the water. I told of how he had come back up to gather their things without her and seemed calm and relaxed. I also told of the terrible night that he tried to force me to go with him. I told them how I had fought and gotten away from him.

During the next few weeks, I sat in the court room and listened to everything that was said. I watched as he tried to convince the jury that he was the victim and that he had suffered from abuse and that abuse had caused him to become the man he was. I listened as he tried to convince them that the lady on the beach had tried to kill him. He claimed he had killed her in self-defense and panicked and did not know what to do so he tried to hide it.

I watched and I listened and I prayed. I was not sure what was going to happen, but I did know that if the other ladies who had gone through so much more than I had were able to sit in that court room and face him, then surely, I could try to do something to help the ones who had not made it. I could try to tell my story to help put him away. And it worked.

The attorneys finished by giving their closing statements. As they spoke, he continued to look at each of us as if to say that he knew he would be freed and that he would come back to hurt us. He was wrong. He was sentenced to a life sentence without parole, and he will never be on the South Carolina beaches again. We would never have to hear of or think of Mr. Stanley Stevens again.

The next summer, we went back to the beach. We stayed in the same house, and we sat out on the strand at the same spot. We watched the children play in the sand and the people enjoying the water. We watched as people walked by. Everyone seemed happy and everyone seemed safe. Though the year before had been one that affected us in ways that we would not know for some time to come, we knew that this year we were back at the beach we loved. We were back on the sunny beach of South Carolina.

I often wondered what would have happened if I had seen the lady and known that she was in trouble. I often wondered what could have happened if the man had known that I had recognized him when he walked up to me. As I thought of that lady, I also thought of this man. I wondered what would have happened to him if his life had been different. Each night before going to sleep, I thanked God that I was okay, and I asked God to forgive him and to work in his life. Each night I prayed that nobody will ever go through something like this again.

But for now, I sit on the beach, I watch the wonderful creation that God has given us, and I am thankful for the calming feeling of sitting on our South Carolina beach.

The Adventure to Matthew's Island

"David, Mary, it's time to get up. Breakfast is ready, and it is time to go outside and play. Where are your adventures taking you today?"

David comes running into the kitchen. "We are going to an island. Matthew is taking us to his own private island. He says that there won't be anyone else there, and there is lots to do."

Mary comes in. "Mom, we have to hurry. The plane is waiting on us to take us to the island. Matthew will be waiting on us. He is taking us to a dessert island."

"That's deserted, not dessert. But anyway, hurry up, Mary."

"Okay, guys, it seems like you two have already planned out your day. I hope it is a great adventure. Remember all the details so you can tell me about it when you get back."

During the summer months, the children loved being outside. As they played, I went about my household duties. I could watch them from the windows and see them as they went on the imaginary adventures that Matthew took them on. The yard had a six-foot privacy fence surrounding it. They enjoyed being outside and were safe. I knew that at the end of each of David's adventures, the children would come back inside and tell me all the details about where they had been without ever leaving the yard. They would have traveled the world and described places in great detail and with great accuracy. Some of his adventures were quite interesting and would make you think that they had actually gone with Matthew.

After playing for a while, they came inside, and I fixed lunch. We sat at the table and talked about our morning.

"Mary, tell me where your brother took you today. Did you have a good adventure?"

"We went to a big island. Nobody else was there. It was just Matthew, David, and me. There were lots of trees and monkeys and animals and you could see through the water. There was a great big beach with lots of shells. Matthew and David went swimming in the ocean."

"Yeah, you could see the bright-colored fish swimming right beside us. Matthew reached down and touched one of them."

David continued. "Mary, it was not just *any* island, it was the Land of Matthew. Don't you remember? We named it after Matthew. He is the one who always tells us where to go. He is the one that takes us on all of our adventures."

"I forgot. Okay, Mom, it was not a deserted island, it was the Land of Matthew."

As we ate our lunch, the children continued to tell me every detail of their adventure. My eight-year-old boy had an imagination that could take him and his six-year-old sister to all the places in the world and to some places that were not even in this world. Today they were visiting the "Land of Matthew." They climbed tall trees so that they could see far away. They ate berries off of bushes and drank water from a spring coming out of the side of a hill. They swam in the ocean where the water was clear enough to see through. The story continued until they had each fallen asleep for an afternoon nap.

A couple of hours later, they were up and ready to go. We all three went outside. I was sitting by the pool watching as David ran around playing and waiting on Mary to go with him on their next adventure.

"Come on, Mary. Let's go. It's time to meet Matthew and go back to the island."

"You go by yourself, David. I don't want to go. I want to stay here with Mama."

David was trying to get Mary to play, but she wanted to sit by the pool. I was sitting close by, so I could hear what they were saying. At first, I thought she had not gotten a good nap, but as the afternoon went on, she still was not playing. She came over to sit with me. I felt her head, and she was burning up with fever.

"Mary, are you not feeling well? You have a fever. I think we need to go inside." I called to David, and we all went inside. By the time we got in, Mary was sweating, shivering, and her fever was 103 degrees. I gave her some Tylenol to try to get her fever down. After another hour had passed, her fever had gone up, and she was beginning to act as if she did not know me.

I called my neighbor to come and take care of David, and I rushed Mary to the hospital. The nurse in the ER saw her and took her straight back to an examine room. The doctor came in immediately. I could tell that she was very concerned.

"Have you and your family been anywhere out of the States lately? Or have you been in a heavily wooded area?" She continued to check Mary. "How long has Mary been sick?"

"No, we have been home all summer. Our yard has a couple of trees, but we have not been into the woods hiking or camping. Most of the summer, they have played in the backyard. She and her brother were playing this morning as they normally do. She seemed quiet after her nap and did not want to play.

I noticed the fever about three o'clock. It was not going down, so I decided to bring her in."

"No, Mama, tell her about our adventure this morning. Tell her about our island," Mary insisted.

"I'm sorry, she does seem to get things confused when she and her brother go on their adventures. They go on 'adventures' with my son's imaginary friend, Matthew. These adventures take them to all parts of the world. Today they went to an island where no people live."

As we were talking, she pulled up Mary's top, and there was now a red rash all over her chest. That had not been there before we left the house. There was also a spot on her ear that looked like an insect bite. The nurse drew blood and had it tested for everything she could think of. The test results did not show anything. With every passing hour, Mary was getting worse, so they took her to the pediatric ICU unit.

When the doctor came back in the room, she seemed even more concerned. "I would suggest that you contact any family that you need to. I am not sure that Mary is going to be okay. Perhaps it would be a good idea if you had someone here with you."

"Her father is out of town. He will be back late tonight. My parents live two hours from here. Their dad's parents are no longer living so it's just my parents and my ex-husband. Do you think they should come now?"

"It would be a good idea for you to go ahead and make those calls."

I went out into the courtyard of the hospital to make a few calls. I called my parents first.

"Mom, this is Marie. Mary is sick. She is really sick, and I don't think she is going to make it. Mom, I need you to come now."

I knew it would be a while before they were here. I called the neighbor who was with David and asked her to bring him to the hospital so they could check him in case whatever Mary had was contagious.

I made one last phone call. "Tom, it's Marie. Tom, I am sorry to call you at work, but something is wrong with Mary. We are at the hospital, and the doctors are not sure what is going on. They said I should call anyone who might need to know. Can you come now? Tom, our Mary may not make it. I need you."

"I am leaving now. Someone else can finish up the meeting, and the jet will be ready when I get to the airport. I should be there in three hours. Hang in there, Marie. I will be home as soon as I can. Mary will be okay. I just know that she will. Don't worry. Where is David? Is David okay?

"David is with the neighbors. They are bringing him up here so the doctors can check him out too."

Tom had the company jet ready when he got to the airport and arrived about three hours later. My parents arrived shortly afterwards. David and I were still waiting in the ICU waiting area. They would not let us go in the back because they were still not sure what was going on. Mary had slipped into a coma and would not know if I was there.

They would give us frequent updates about her condition. Each time they came out, it seemed as if the news was getting worse. One time they asked where the children had been that day. David started to tell them of their adventures and how the stack of firewood had been their obstacle course that they had to climb to get through their training before their trip. The doctor asked if she could check David to make sure he did not have any bite marks or ticks. They did not find anything on him, and he continued to seem fine.

By midnight, we were all tired, and David needed to be home. Tom drove my parents and David back to our house and got them settled in. They allowed me to sit by Mary's bed and hold her hand. Even though she was in a coma, I wanted her to know that I was there with her. Her fever had gone down a little, and she seemed to be resting.

"God, I don't know if you are there or not. I know it has been a long time since we have talked, but God, please don't take Mary away from me. I can't lose her too. God, I will do anything if you will just save our little girl. Please, God, please let her come back to us."

The night shift doctor came in to make rounds. As he was looking at her, he noticed a spot at the top of her ear that seemed swollen. "Has this spot been like this all day?"

"It was there when the doctor first examined Mary, but it was very small and more of a pink color. It seems more swollen and darker now, and it seems to be spreading."

"This looks like a spider bite, and I want to do some more blood work to find out what kind of spider it was. I have just come back from a mission trip to an island where there had been an outbreak of insect bites that had caused very similar reactions. I will have the technician come in and draw the blood."

They put a rush on the results, and within two hours, we had the information they were looking for. Mary had indeed been bitten by an insect. This was a deadly insect, and if we had not been there with her to get her to the hospital when we did we probably would have lost her. They began a different type of antibiotic and put her in total isolation. They allowed Tom and me to go into the room for a few minutes at a time and to sit with her and talk with her. We needed to make sure that she stayed calm and quiet at all times.

"Mary, Mama and Daddy are here with you. I am not sure if you can hear me or not, but we love you. You are going to be okay. We need you to come back to us. Can you hear us, Mary?" We would sit and tell her we loved her over and over again so that she would be able to hear our voices.

"Marie, while we are here alone, I just want to tell you that you have been a good mother. I have never stopped loving you or the children. I just was not able to deal with the first loss that we had the way you did. I could not live every day pretending that he was not a part of us. I am sorry that I have not been there for you and the kids like you wanted me too."

"Tom, I know, and I have never stopped loving you. I had to pretend that he was not a part of my life or I could never have gone on. It was not fair to you. I hope that one day you will forgive me. You have always provided for us, and you have been there when we needed you."

"Marie, there is nothing to forgive. We can only pray that we don't lose Mary, too. I have gone back to church, and I know that prayers can and do work. Marie, we have to trust that God will do a miracle in Mary's life. We have to trust in Him."

The nurse that had been with us came in. "I am sorry, but it is time for visitors to leave. You will be able to come back in after the shift change."

Tom and I walked back out of the ICU unit feeling more desperate than before. While we were sitting in the waiting room, we heard an emergency call. All the nurses and doctors in the unit were running to a room. It was Mary's room. She was having seizures and was jerking and shaking. Her jerking was so strong that the bed was moving. Her head had swollen to about twice the normal size, and her face was a deep spotted red. The doctors did not know we were listening, but we knew what was about to happen. We were losing our daughter.

I begged them to let me go in and sit with her. My thought was that if I was there, she may be calmer. I knew that if it was contagious, that I had already been exposed, and so I could not see the danger of me being there. After me begging and pleading, they allowed Tom and me to sit with her. I sat and held her hand for the rest of the night. I watched her face, and from time to time, it seemed as if she would look toward the window and smile.

That was the beginning of our new routine. This routine went on for several days. My parents would take care of David and take turns coming to the hospital to see us. Tom and I would sit by Mary's bed and hold her hand and talk to her. People from Tom's church would come and visit and were wonderful about taking food to the house so that my mother would not have to cook. Neighbors and friends called and visited, and each one offered prayers for Mary's recovery. It seemed as if this was going to be our new life.

On the fourth day, Mary's fever was down, and the rash was beginning to go away. The swelling in her face was down, and the spot on her ear was fading. She was still in a coma, and the doctors were telling us that we still were not out of the woods yet. I was hopeful that all of these good signs were signs that she would have a full recovery. She was only six years old. She deserved to have a normal life. And besides I could not lose another child. I had lost Matthew when he was born, and I was not going to lose Mary.

They were having revival at Tom's church that week. One night, a church member went up front and told Mary's story to the congregation. The pastor decided not to have his normal service. Instead they began a twenty-four-hour prayer vigil.

A group of people would take a time slot, and for the next twenty-four hours, there was not a second that someone was not praying for Mary's recovery. They had contacted Tom and told him of the twenty-four-hour prayer vigil, and they told him that they would continue to pray until we saw a miracle in the life of our family.

The next day was more of the same. The doctors had begun to talk to us about the possibility that Mary may not make a full recovery, and she may be in the hospital for a very long time. They suggested that we begin to make arrangements to have one of us at the hospital at a time and that the rest of us go about our normal routines.

I could not believe that they were saying those words to me. I would not accept anything except a full recovery. Nothing was going to happen to Mary. I was sure of it. It just could not happen twice.

Late that afternoon, my parents brought David up to the hospital. We ate supper together in the waiting room, and we tried to help him understand what was going on.

"Son, Mary was bitten by an insect, and it has made her very sick. She is going to have to be here for quite some time. I am not sure how we are going to work things out, but Grandmama and Granddaddy are going to be with you while Daddy and I are here with Mary."

"Don't worry about it, Mama. Matthew has already told me that Mary is going to be okay. He said it today when we went on our adventure. He took me back to the island to tell me all kinds of things about who he was."

"David, now is not the time for your imaginary friend. This is real. You need to listen to me. Stop talking about imaginary friends and adventures and listen to what I am saying."

"I am, Mama, but Matthew said—"

"David, stop."

It was about eight o'clock in the evening when the nurse came running through the door of the ICU unit. "Come quickly. Come see your little girl."

At first, I was afraid that they were telling us to come quickly to be able to tell her goodbye. My parents, David, Tom, and I ran into the room. We knew that David was not allowed, but we also knew that when we went running in with him and they did not stop us, that had to mean something.

We got to her room and saw Mary sitting up in the bed, talking to everyone around her. She looked over at us and said she knew we had been there, and she was sorry she had made us cry. She said she was glad that Mama and Daddy still loved each other, and she wanted Daddy to come back home. She then started telling us the story of what had happened to her. Not only was she out of the coma and her fever gone, she seemed like her old self. She was telling us all about her adventure. It sounded so much like one of David's adventures that we all listened to her, knowing that she would take us on the journey with her.

She told us that she and David had gotten on a plane and had flown to a deserted island, and while she was trying to find food, a big strange looking bug came up and tried to bite her. The bug flew up and landed on her head and bit her ear. But then she grabbed it and stomped it. She took care of that bug.

She said that she remembered that she had started to feel bad so David had gotten her into the plane, and they had flown back home and gone inside to eat and take a nap. But that was really all she remembered until she got to the hospital.

She continued to tell us of her stay in the hospital. She had been in a coma the whole time, yet she told us of almost every detail that had happened. She said that there was a beautiful lady who came and stood by her. It was the lady in the picture on our mantle that was standing next to her daddy. That lady had told her that she wanted to take her to the most beautiful place in the world and that she had someone special for her to meet. Mary continued her story of how this lady told her that she was her grandmother and that she was so nice and that she had taken her to meet Jesus. Jesus had held her and talked to her for a long time. He told her that it was not quite time for her to come live with Him, so he was going to ask her to go back home to her mama and daddy and stay with them for a while. He told her about her other brother, too. He told her that Matthew was with him and that he was okay.

"Mama, why don't you talk about Matthew? Why didn't you tell us he was our brother? It makes him sad to know that you miss him so much. But he said to tell you that he is okay and he loves all of us and he is always with us."

The tears began to flow. "I couldn't tell you. It was something that I did not want to talk about. Daddy and I had a child before David was born. He had not lived but a few hours, and I had told my family that I just could not talk about him. We had never told you about your older brother because it hurt too much."

Mary described Matthew just as I had imagined him. He would be ten years old now. He would have looked a lot like David, and he would have had his daddy's eyes.

"His name is Matthew and he is always with us and he is the one that takes us on our adventures. It was his way of still being a part of our family. I got to play with him while I was not here. He told me that he was always there on David's wild adventures."

David spoke up and said, "I told you that I always felt like I had someone with me but just did not know who it was. And now you tell me I have a brother named Matthew. The same Matthew from my adventures. Wow. I don't know what is going on here."

The doctors and nurses had been in the room listening to her story. One of the nurses happen to mention that is was eight o'clock exactly when she just sat up and started talking. My parents, Tom, and I looked at each other in amazement. Tom simply said, "Twenty-four hours."

That was all that needed to be said. Everyone in the room knew what had just happened. We had truly witnessed a miracle. We saw prayer working. The night before, at exactly eight o'clock was when the prayer vigil began. For twenty-four hours, prayers had been prayed, and at the end of that time, we had our miracle.

The next morning, we were sitting in the room when the nurse came in. "All of the lab reports came back completely normal. Mary seems to be back to herself. The doctor will be in shortly to talk with you."

The doctor that had diagnosed Mary came by to see her with a picture of an insect. "Did the insect that you saw look anything like the one in the picture?"

Mary smiled. "Yes, but my insect was a lot bigger. But I stomped it."

The doctor looked at Tom and me and continued, "This insect is a very rare spider that is only found on an island and has never been known to be in the United States. We can never be sure how it got into your backyard."

I explained, "I think we know. I think it was God's way of bringing our family back together. He knew our family needed to deal with the loss of Matthew, and He knew how to get my attention."

Tom smiled. "I don't know how it happened, but the only explanation that we can give you is that David and Mary had gone on an adventure to a deserted island with their brother Matthew. Mary was bitten by a rare spider and became very ill. She went to Heaven with a beautiful angel that looked like my mother and she met her older brother and she was able to sit on Jesus's lap and talk to Him. Jesus told her that she needed to come back home for a while longer, so she did."

"Well, Tom, that sounds like as good of an explanation as I could give."

Tom moved back home the following month, and we went to his church as a family. Our family was able to talk about Matthew any time that we wanted to. We continued to hear of the adventures that David and Mary and Matthew would go on. As they grew older, David did not talk of the adventures, but Mary always held them close to her heart.

David and Mary are now adults with families of their own. David is an airline pilot and flies all over the world. David's son continues to go on adventures just as his father had. He also has an imaginary friend named Matthew who travels the world with him.

Mary is now a pediatric critical care nurse. Mary has a little girl who travels the world to imaginary places and has her own great adventures with Matthew. We sit quietly and listen to every adventure and listen to them share their stories. We cherish each story, but the adventure that we will never forget is the adventure of David and Mary and of course, Matthew and the deserted island. The story of the adventures that Mary had following their trip in the ICU unit always follows.

Rick's Place

My mother taught us that no matter what, there was always room at our table for one more. I do not think that she was talking about animals. However, in our family, it seems as if every week, there is a new stray to feed. I wonder if somehow the word is out that we will not turn an animal away, so everyone comes to the edge of our property and drops off unwanted animals.

As of today, we have five humans, three horses, ten dogs, twelve cats, and a variety of farm animals that I would not begin to count. I have told the children time after time not to get too attached to them. It is our goal to find each one of them a forever home. However, there is one exception. That is with our little mixed dog that weighs about twenty pounds. He is an older dog who wondered up into the yard, walked over to where our five-year-old daughter was sitting, crawled up into her lap, and fell asleep. I do not understand that bond, but it is not one that I argue with. I know that as long as he is around, nobody is going to come near her.

We live in a rural area where there is lots of land for the children to explore. Our older children, who are twelve-year-old twins, often leave their little sister behind. They think that she will slow them down and not be able to keep up. She is often left in the backyard crying. Sam is always close by. He seems to know that she needs him as much as he needs her.

All summer long, the first summer he was with us, their bond continued to grow. One night, Sam slipped past us and spent the night in the house. I found him lying next to Jenny with her arms around him the next morning. I have never quite known how he managed to do it, but for a few nights straight, he would get in, and we would find him in Jenny's bed. Finally we gave in and let him become a house dog. Jenny and Sam were both very happy with our decision. Wherever you would see one, you would always see the other.

When the leaves began to change colors, we were out in the yard. "Jenny, have you noticed that the leaves on some of the trees are starting to change colors? The leaves have their own way of telling us that the seasons are changing. During the Fall, the leaves turn yellow, orange, brown, dark red, and other colors too. They then fall to the ground. This is one of God's ways of showing us that the weather will soon be changing. Would you like to gather up the pretty leaves and put them in a book like I did when I was your age?"

Jenny replied with excitement, "Can we, Mom? Can Sam and I go out and get leaves?"

We walked around our property, gathering pretty colored leaves and took them home and ironed them between two pieces of wax paper—the way I had done as a child.

I noticed that she seemed to keep looking at the leaves during the afternoon. I wondered what was going on that little mind of hers. After we had finished supper, she asked me if she could play in the backyard until dark. I told her that she could as long as her brothers were out there, but as soon as they came in, she had to come in with them.

After about an hour, I went to get them in for the night. "Boys, where are Jenny and Sam?

"We don't know. We have been working on our treehouse since supper. She is probably back inside."

"Jenny, Sam, where are you? Answer me please. It's too late to play hide and seek. Come on, Jenny, let's go inside."

She did not answer. We started searching the yard. She was not inside the fence. My heart began to race, and I had so many things running through my head. The boys were out there when she walked outside. They were working on their new treehouse. I thought that she would stay close by. But when we could not find her or Sam, I knew that she had gone into the woods. She had wondered off to find more leaves.

She was only five years old. She would not know how to protect herself or to get food or water. The night would be scary and cold. We called all of our neighbors and friends and began to look for her. We searched for hours. Each person took a different part of the property to search. We had our cellphones to get in touch with each other.

One by one, our neighbors told us it was too dark to continue so we decided to start again in the morning. Greg and I did not give up. We continued looking all night. We searched every inch of the open area of the property. That could only mean that Jenny had gone into the woods. And if she was in the woods, so was Sam. Sam would be next to her and would hear us calling and would bark. That was our only hope.

The next morning, all of our friends and neighbors were back. The search continued all morning. About one o'clock, I received a telephone call. One of our friends had seen something, and I should get there as soon as I could. Greg and I got there about the same time. It looked as if someone had a fire going and had been camping out on our property. Every possible thought that you could imagine was going through our brains. First, where was the person that had been camping here? Why was someone on our property and had this person done something to our little girl and her dog? We needed answers.

"Greg, did you know someone was camping here? I have my dog with me." Our neighbor said, "We could see if he could get a scent from whoever is here and see if he can track him down." He did just that. He started barking and running toward the stream about a mile away. We followed as quickly as we could.

"I'll call 911 and have them out here before you get back. Just in case we need it, that is. I will stay here and wait on them. Call me as soon as you find her, so I can take them to you," one of our neighbor said.

We finally made it to the stream. There was no sign of Jenny or Sam, but there was a young man with a fishing pole. He seemed to be unable to speak and was very frightened at the sight of us. Because this area of the property had been closed off for years, we did not know he had been camping here for several months.

Greg approached him first. The boy started to run. He was stopped by one of our neighbors. It was obvious by the scars on his back that he had been abused.

"Who are you? Where is Jenny? Where is Sam? You better tell me now or we will call the police." Greg was angry, and you could see that the boy's expression showed he knew what anger was like. He would not answer any of our questions and seemed to be unable to speak.

When he saw me, he walked over to me and touched my face. He looked sad and turned away. He looked back again and did the same thing. But this time when he touched my face, he put his hand as to show my height and then down lower. I realized he was trying to ask if I was the little girl's mother.

"Are you trying to tell me that you have seen Jenny and Sam? Do you know where they are?" I questioned him about seeing her. He never spoke. But he kept motioning with his hands. We were trying to figure out what he was trying to tell us.

Greg asked, "Have you seen my little girl that looks like her mother?"

He nodded. After a number of questions, we realized that he must have been watching our house since he was camping out in the woods. He was trying to ask us if we were looking for the little girl that looked like her mother.

There was a part of our property that had been closed off for years. Some of the local churches had used it for retreats and summer youth camps. After a hurricane had come through and destroyed the building, we closed it up and never thought of it. It was in the back part of the property and not near the road we normally traveled.

The boy kept pointing in that direction. He knew where it was. He took us straight to it. He went as far as he could but would not go out into the open area. Everyone else spread out and started searching the area. One after another came back to tell us that they had not found her. Then the young boy seemed to get excited. He was motioning and making a strange noise.

I went over to him. "Can you show me?" Will you point me in the right direction?"

He pointed to the old bunk house that was falling in. We did not know if he had seen something or not, but it was worth looking in to. Greg went in first. The floor had caved in in parts of the room. But he could hear something. He followed the sound.

"Jenny, honey, are you in here? Sam, where are you?" It was an all too familiar sound. It was Sam. Sam was hurt. He had fallen through the floor, and Jenny was asleep next to the hole he had slipped in to. As we got closer, Sam was growling and barking as to still try to protect Jenny.

Jenny woke up when she heard him and saw us there. She ran into Greg's arms and started crying.

"Sam got hurt. Sam is hurt. Daddy, I can't get him. Daddy, you have to get Sam."

"Okay, Jenny, we can get Sam, but first I have to get you out of here. I will take you to Mama. She is right outside. Then I will come back in and get Sam."

We were able to get Sam out of the hole and get everyone else out before the building caved in some more. The boy that had shown us the way had disappeared. We could find no trace of him.

Sam was taken to the vet, and Jenny was taken to the hospital. After Sam had been released, we were allowed to take him to the hospital to see Jenny. We opened the front door of the hospital, and he jumped out of Greg's arms. He took off down the hall to Jenny's room. He jumped up on her bed and laid down next to her.

The doctors were concerned about Jenny because she seemed very confused and kept talking about the boy that would not talk. We told the doctors what had happened during our search for her and that there indeed was a boy that would not talk.

We knew that Jenny was too young to know what had happened.

"Jenny, did you see anyone in the woods?"

"Mama, I told you. I saw the boy that would not talk. He was in the woods by himself. He was crying." She did not want to bother him, so she kept walking.

"I got lost and couldn't remember how to get back. It was getting dark, and I was starting to get scared. Sam was brave though. He stayed right with me. It was almost dark, and that's when I saw the boy that would not talk. I asked him to help me. He didn't say anything, but he took me to a big opened area and pointed to the shed. Sam and I started to walk across the field, but the boy did not come. He wouldn't leave the woods. He just kept pointing toward the shed. I figured out he was trying to tell me to go into the building. So Sam and I went inside. That is when Sam fell through the floor. I couldn't leave him, so I stayed. I stayed all night until I fell asleep. I was going to go get you when it got light, but you found me before I woke up. That boy saved Sam and me."

Jenny spent one more night in the hospital to make sure that she was okay. After she got home, she kept asking about the boy that would not talk. We wanted to know about him too. Who was he? How could he have been camping on our property and we not know about it? How could he have known that I had a little girl that looked like me? This was all very strange.

I began to research to find out if anyone knew of a boy who would be about fifteen years old that would have big scars on his back like he had been beaten. Nobody in town or any of the surrounding towns knew anything about him. I started searching online. I searched for any missing person that would fit his description. There was nothing. Every search took me to a dead end.

About a month later, we went out to supper and were sitting in a restaurant. Jenny noticed a picture of a boy sitting by a creek. "Mama, look. That is the boy. That is the boy that took me to the building. He kept Sam and me safe from the weather that night I got lost."

When the waiter came back to the table, we asked her if she knew who the boy was in the picture. "Oh, that's Bill's son. He left home when he was fifteen, and nobody has ever heard from him again. Bill's other son owns the restaurant now, but he won't let anybody take that picture down. He says it reminds him of the brother he once had."

"Do you think we could speak with him? It is very important." I asked.

The waitress went and got Billy. She told him that we wanted to speak to him about the picture.

When he walked over to the table, we could see the family resemblance.

Jenny blurted out with excitement. "Are you the boy's daddy?"

"No, little girl, that is just a picture of my brother. What is your name?"

"I'm Jenny, and I want to talk with your brother. He saved me and Sam."

"Jenny, you can't talk to him. That picture was taken many years ago when we were teenagers. His name was Rick. He was a couple of years older than me. When he was fifteen, he left home, and we were never able to find him."

"Sir," Greg said softly, "would you sit with us for a few minutes? I want to tell you a story. About a month ago, our daughter Jenny and her dog, Sam, got lost in the woods behind our house. We searched all night for her and finally found her the next day. While we were searching for her, we came across a campfire on our property. We had no idea anyone had been camping out there. The fire was out, but we knew someone had been there. We continued to look for our daughter, and we saw a teenage boy by the creek. The boy looked just like the boy in the picture. He would not speak. He did motion to us and in his own way led us to find Jenny. It was very strange though. He would not step out of the woods. He would only point and then hide back in the woods. My wife and I noticed that his shirt was torn and that his back had huge scars on it."

Billy put his head down and asked, "Did he walk with a limp?"

"Why, yes, I think he did," I said with almost fear in my voice. "What are you telling us? If this was your brother, he would be at least sixty years old now. It cannot be the same person."

Billy continued his story. "I don't like to talk about this in public, but our father was very mean when he was drinking. He ran this restaurant for years, and everyone in town thought he was a good man. But when he would come home and start drinking, he became a monster. My brother was older than me, so he tried to protect me.

"One day, Daddy was beating him pretty bad. I ran out of the house and hid in the barn. When it got dark, and I knew that daddy would be passed out, I went back inside to check on my brother. I could not find him. The next day, Daddy told me that he had run away just like my mama had done. I didn't know where he had gone or how to find him. I searched all the woods around town many times. I found no trace of him.

"After Daddy died, I found out that my mother had indeed run away. I found letters that she had written to him, begging him to let us go to her. She promised that she would never tell anyone that he beat her if she could just have her boys. My daddy had all the letters in a box, but most of them had not been opened. I found an address on the last letter and looked her up. She allowed me to visit her."

"I am so sorry, Billy. This must have been a nightmare for you," I said, trying to comfort him.

"When I saw my mama, she told me how mean he had been, and when I told her about my brother, she told me that I should quit looking for him. She told me the horrible story about one of the few letters she ever received from my father. He had sent her a box. There was piece of paper in the box with only one sentence on it. 'Here's the only part of my boys that you will ever have.' Those were the only words he wrote on that paper. It made me sick to my stomach. The man that I knew as my father had beaten my mother and chased her off. He had beaten my brother to death and thrown his body in the woods after cutting his tongue out to send to my mother. He had never told anyone about it.

"My mother had tried to tell the police, but nobody would believe her because she was known as the crazy lady that showed up in town only wearing a gown and had nothing else with her. She had been hospitalized for years. She tried to get someone to save her boys, but they just thought she was crazy. When she finally was released from the mental hospital, she was too old to travel. She had gone back to the home that she had moved in to when she ran away. They had saved her mail for more than twenty years. It was then that she saw the letter from my daddy. Twenty years after it had all happened.

"It was about that time that the first family came in with a story similar to yours. Each time it is someone in trouble that is helped by a teenage boy that won't speak. Each time he is able to lead people to find the missing person. And each time he refuses to go out of the woods into an open area. "So your little girl was saved by an angel. She was saved by the angel who had protected me from a monster, and she was saved by an angel that had saved so many other people who have been lost."

Jenny replied, "Wait, my friend is an angel? That's why Sam did not bark at him when he helped me. I wondered about that. Can I see him again?"

"No, Jenny," I tried to explain. "We are not able to see angels when we want to. We only see angels when God needs us to. Rick is God's special angel that he lets help people that are lost like you were."

Greg asked, "What about you, Billy? I know that this had to be a very difficult thing for you to share. I hope that it did not bring up too many bad memories for you. Thank you so much for telling us your story. It helps us understand what happened that night."

We went home that night and started to think about the area that had been closed down after the hurricane had destroyed the buildings. We talked about it for a few weeks before we decided that we should open the camp back up. We should open a camp for abused children who are lucky enough to survive the abuse and to get out of the homes where they are abused.

We talked with lawyers and the city council and the organizations that deal with abused children. We got all of our plans together, and work would begin so that the camp would open up the following summer. The camp would be called Rick's Place, and there would be a monument in his memory to remind everyone that not all people survive the abuse and that we should do all that we can to help them before it is too late.

The old campground was cleared out. The creek was cleared out and turned into a lazy river that children could enjoy during their stay at the camp. There would be four dorms. Each would have enough space for eight children and two counselors. Each dorm would have a kitchen and three baths. There would be a huge conference center where groups from all over could come and hold meetings on abuse. The animals that had been dropped off at the house would be taken there and would become part of the healing process. We would have special people to work with the animals and with the children.

The next summer, the camp was complete. All of our plans were in place, and the grand opening was right around the corner. We asked Billy if he would come and help us cut the ribbon. Billy brought his mother to the grand opening. Greg and I welcomed everyone, and Greg shared the story of the night our little girl was lost. He told the story of how Rick had been her hero and that even those that do not believe in God had to know that it was a miracle that she had been saved by an angel.

Billy was very brave and, for the first time in his life, opened up and told the story about who his father really was. During the time he was speaking, he made a surprise announcement. He was closing the restaurant that his father had opened where he had worked since he was a teenager. And if we would have him, he would like to donate his time to be the cook at our camp when we had guest staying there.

Jenny and Sam were there along with our sons. Many of the people who had searched for Jenny that night and the following day were also there. This was a celebration of life and a celebration of what God could do in the life of a town.

Billy's mother passed away a year after the opening. In her will, she left a large endowment to the camp. The lady that everyone had assumed was homeless and crazy had actually been from a very wealthy family and had been left a lot of money that had been held in a trust for her. Once she had been released from the hospital and had contacted her family, she was told of the trust but she had never touched it. That trust has allowed many young boys and girls to spend time at the camp who otherwise would not be able to afford it.

Billy has become part of our extended family. He joins us for holidays and family get togethers.

The boys are now teenagers and work at the camp every summer. Jenny and Sam continue their bond, and they spend a lot of their time during the summer, floating down the creek that was turned into a lazy river.

Greg and I continue to find strays that have been left on our property. These are sent to the camp to be trained as service animals.

We had no idea that one day, a little girl playing outside would wonder off to find more leaves to match the color of the ones she had found earlier would lead us to such an adventure. The scariest night and day of our lives has led to the most wonderful adventure we could have imagined. Rick's Place will continue to flourish and will continue to help children feel safe and happy, and it will help them know that they can live through the abuse and become strong and healthy adults.

Changed Lives

The summer of 1968 began like most other summers. Ed and Nan would visit their families in North Carolina and South Carolina before heading back home to their home on the east coast of South Carolina. They had been visiting Nan's sister, Beth and her husband, Charlie.

"Bye, son. We will see you in a couple of weeks. We will miss you. Have fun." These would be the last words that Eddie would hear from his mother.

Their eight-year-old son wanted to stay and play with his cousins. It was summer, and it would be a great time for these boys to be together. Ed and Nan were not excited about leaving him but knew that it would be good for each of them. They had twin daughters that were almost a year old, and they thought that Eddie would like time to be with his cousins instead of always having to be there to help with his sisters. As Ed and Nan drove away, they waved to Eddie and as always did the sign language sign for "I love you."

Ed was driving, and Nan was reading the map, trying to find a nearby sightseeing adventure to visit on their way home. The twins were asleep in the backseat. They were just miles away from the border of South Carolina and Georgia. This was not in the original plans, but since Ed did not have to be back at work for another week, they made a spur of the moment decision to visit the mountains of Georgia. There were several restaurants along the way where they could stop and get the girls something to eat before starting this new adventure.

"Ed, I wish that Eddie was with us. He would like to see the mountains. It seems strange without him. I wonder if he misses us yet."

"Nan, you are always worried about your children. You and I know that Eddie is having the time of his life. He is eight years old, and I am sure that Beth is making him feel like a king. But I do wish someone knew we were not going straight home. Maybe we should have used the pay phone at the diner to call Beth."

Ed continued to drive, and Nan was doing the navigating. She saw a sign that pointed them to a less traveled road that would take them to Look Out Mountain. Surely they could find a place to stay there.

Ed turned right and began to follow the signs to their destination. There was very little traffic on the road. Ed and Nan were talking about how quiet it was with the girls once again asleep and Eddie not being there to ask how much longer it would take to get to the motel.

Suddenly, Ed slammed on brakes. The car was making a very loud noise, and he wanted to stop before something happened. It was too late. The car suddenly exploded, and the family was unable to get out.

A man passing by drove as fast as he could to the nearest store and called the police. The police and fire department would arrive within just a few minutes. The crowd had gathered around the car but knew to stay back. Some cars were pulling away while others remained. The car had exploded so the fire department knew there was nothing they could do for the people inside. They would put the fire out and hope that there was enough evidence available to find out who the people were.

Unfortunately there was not. The explosion had destroyed everything. There seemed to be the remains of two people in the front seat. There was no evidence of anyone else in the car. As the crowd left, and the police and firemen were leaving, someone heard a faint cry.

A nurse that was going home after her shift ran to where the cry was coming from. It was a young girl. She seemed to be about a year old and was not talking yet. The nurse traveled back to the hospital with the infant. She stayed with her when she was not on duty and checked on her during the days she was working.

This nurse, a single young lady, asked if she could take the child as her foster parent while they looked for her family. The nurse was Miss Suzanne. She had always planned on having a family but did not know it would come about this way. Suzanne was granted rights to keep this little girl. She would be her foster mom until her family was found.

Weeks went by without any word. The local television station began airing information to try to find out who these people were as soon as the wreck happened. There seemed to be nobody looking for this family of three, and there seemed to be no answers during the police investigations.

After a week had passed, Eddie was sitting near the phone, waiting to hear from his parents. They did not call. His aunt and uncle tried to reassure him that everything was okay, and perhaps there was a problem with the phone. They told him that his parents would call as soon as possible. They did not.

Beth decided to go to the police and see if she could file a missing person's report. She did, and the news channels in the area were posting pictures and stating that they were looking for a family of four. They put pictures out for everyone to see. The newspapers also published the stories. Nothing was ever heard.

The family knew that this was unlike Ed and Nan, but they had no clue as to what had happened. After a month, they began to think that the search was not going to find them. Summer would soon be coming to an end, and Eddie would need to be back in school. It was decided that Beth and Charlie would be given temporary custody of Eddie, and he would go to school with their boys.

Months turned into years. Eddie always felt that his parents had deserted him and taken his two sisters and run away. He felt unloved and unwanted, and he always felt as if he just did not belong. His family did all they could to help him feel otherwise, but he would not listen.

Eddie was given every advantage that a young man could ask for. He was in the best schools. He participated in sports and other school activities. He was treated as a son and was loved very much by his Aunt Beth and her family. He had been able to go to college and was now working in his uncle's company and was a successful and well-known young man.

The little girl was adopted by Nurse Suzanne and raised as her own. Suzanne made sure to always let her know what had happened and how she had come to live with her. Even though there were no details, she wanted Amy to know that she did have a family and that her parents did not just leave her or give her up for adoption.

Amy and Suzanne had a wonderful life. They were not wealthy, and they did not have an easy time financially, but Suzanne gave Amy every opportunity to be the best she could be. She had gone to a good school and had just graduated from high school. She was able to enroll in a college nearby and would be living on campus. It would not be long before she would be entering this new world, and it would be the first time that she would ever remember being away from Suzanne. The time was getting close, and she was not sure if she was ready for college.

Ready or not, the school year was about to begin. Suzanne drove her to school and helped her get her dorm room set up. She left and went back home. There was the normal time for adjustment, but Amy was on her way. However, there was one thing that continued to happen that concerned her. She was often confused for someone else. It seemed as if she was often called Ann. She would tell them that her name was Amy and that she did not know Ann. Each person would tell her that she looked just like another girl on campus. Amy did not quite know how to take this. She tried to be polite each time someone called her Ann. She had come to believe that Ann must be a much more social person than she was. Ann seemed to be known all over campus.

One day, Amy was walking into the library at the same time another student was walking out. She was stopped in her tracks. The person in front of her looked just like her. She thought this must be Ann.

She said, "Hello, Ann. We finally meet. I have been called Ann so many times that I was beginning to wonder if I had forgotten my own name. But I always have my necklace with my name on it to tell me who I am."

"You must be Amy." Ann laughed. "I have been getting the same thing. You sure do look a lot like me. Where are you from?"

Amy answered, "I live just about two hours away in a small town in Georgia. How about you? Are you from around here?"

"Well, that is a little strange too. I live just about two hours away too. I live in South Carolina. I guess the school is about halfway between our hometowns. Have you always lived in Georgia?" answered Ann.

Amy replied, "Well, for as long as I can remember. It is a long story, but I was adopted when I was about a year old, and I don't know anything about where my birth family is. What about you?

Ann continued with her story. "Well. it is just me and my mom. My mom was not married, and she was young when I was born. It has just been the two of us all my life. We don't see her family at all. I have never met my grandparents or even heard much about them. So yeah, I guess I have always been right where we live now. Mom just won't talk about it. I wish she would so that I could meet my grandparents and find out who my father was. Hey, look at us. We sure are sharing a lot of personal stuff not to have ever met before. But I feel like I have known you all my life."

Amy laughed. "Me too, me too. This is unreal. Let's get together this weekend and talk again. I can't wait to tell my mom about this."

During the first semester at school, the girls became good friends. Amy asked her mom if she could invite Ann and her mother to spend Thanksgiving with them. They were always by themselves, and she really wanted her to meet Ann. Suzanne agreed and made sure that she would be off for a couple of days so they could all spend time together.

Ann spoke to her mother. Her mother hesitated and acted a little strange, but after Ann insisted, Dottie finally agreed and made plans to go to Georgia for Thanksgiving. After all, she too was curious to meet this girl that looked like a mirror image of her daughter. Secretly she was scared to find out the truth because she thought she already knew what would happen when they met.

When Thanksgiving break came, the girls drove to Amy's house. Dottie would meet them there Thursday morning. Dottie arrived early, and the four ladies began the meal preparations and spent time in the kitchen getting to know each other.

Looking at the girls was really like looking at the same person. Suzanne spoke up. "I have always heard the old saying that everyone has a twin in this world, but I never thought I would meet my daughter's twin. This is unbelievable."

Dottie agreed. "It is very strange. If I saw Amy somewhere, I would think it was Ann. And each of their names starts with an A. That is just one more thing."

"It is," Suzanne continued. "I don't know if Amy has told Ann or not, but I am not Ann's biological mother. I was working in a hospital when one night on my way home, I came up on a terrible wreck. The fire department tried but could not find any evidence as to who the people were. It appeared to be a man and a woman in the front street and no sign of anyone else. I heard a baby crying. An officer and I walked toward the cry, and that is where we found Amy. She was shaken up, but she was okay. We took her to the hospital and tried to find some of her family. Nobody ever came forward.

"The Georgia newspapers and local television stations did stories on her for a while. Each story always included a picture of a little one-year-old girl wearing a necklace with her name on it. After nobody came forward, I was given an opportunity to adopt her. I had taken her home from the hospital as a foster parent and fell in love with her. I just knew she had to be my daughter."

Amy walked over to Suzanne and gave her a hug. "And she has been the best mother that any child could have ever asked for. I wish I knew a little about my history, but she is my mom, and that is all I need to know."

Ann spoke up, "Wow, what a story. She said she was adopted, but she never told me the whole story. It's always just been me and my mom, and I have never met my family either. I know that it has been hard on her, but I love her so much and she has been a great mother."

Dottie spoke up. "That is enough of this talk. Let's get this meal fixed and enjoy the afternoon."

Dottie became very quiet for the rest of the day, and it was obvious that she was thinking about something. After lunch, the girls went out to the mall to do some early Christmas shopping. They wanted to get just the right dresses for their first college dance. This gave Suzanne and Dottie a chance to talk.

"Dottie, I noticed that you got quiet while we were talking about the girls. Are you okay? I know it has been hard being a single mom and not having the support of your family. I was lucky that my family lived close by, and Amy has always known them as her grandparents. Do you mind me asking where Ann's father is?" Suzanne asked.

"Well, I have always been a single mom. He has never been a part of our lives. I wish I could have married and given her a father, but it just did not work out that way," Dottie sadly replied.

"I know that Ann has been loved and has been given everything she needs. All you have to do is look at the two of you and you see the love you share. I never married either. I dated a few people, but it never felt right. Amy has done fine without having a father in her life, and it seems as if Ann has too. I am very glad these two found each other at school."

The girls were having a great time at the mall. They tried on a number of dresses, and every time they went into a store, the clerks referred to them as twins. They laughed and never said anything to correct the clerks. But it did make them start wondering. What if somehow, they really were related? Their birthdays were just a few weeks apart and they really did have some very similar characteristics and besides they looked just alike. What if somehow, they were actually related? They talked all afternoon about it.

When they got back to Amy's house, they decided to ask their moms if they could do one of the new DNA tests to see where they came from.

Suzanne was fine with it. She said she knew people who could help but that it would cost quite a bit of money. She would have to check in to that part first. Dottie, on the other hand, was upset and very much against it. She wanted no part of it and told Ann that she was not allowed to have the test done.

Ann was shocked by her mother's response and asked, "Mom, what's wrong? I have never seen you act like this before. Why does my finding out more about our family bother you so much? It won't change who we are. It will just mean that I might know a little more about who my daddy was and where he came from. It could be a good thing. And what if somewhere down the line Amy and I really are related? Wouldn't that be great?"

Dottie yelled angrily, "Ann, I said no, and I do not want to ever hear anything else about it! Do you hear me? Never speak of this again." Dottie stormed off to the guest room, leaving the other three sitting in disbelief. They did not understand her response but knew that they could not go further with this without her permission. DNA test had been around for only a short time and were only used in special cases. At this time, the possibility of knowing anything about your past from DNA was just beginning to be used, and nobody they knew had experience with it. Perhaps Dottie was just afraid of the test and the unknown.

Dottie went back to South Carolina the next day, and the girls headed back to college. The conversation was not discussed again until the girls got back to school. Suzanne went back to work the following Monday. She decided to follow through with the idea of the DNA testing and find out what the process would be and if it was possible to tell if the girls were related without having Dottie involved. The girls were over eighteen, so they would not need parental consent.

After talking with the people in the hospital lab, Suzanne decided that if the girls wanted to do this, then she would find a way to pay for it. She knew she did not need to be tested because she was not biologically related to Amy. They may not be able to get family history from Dottie, but they would know if they were distantly related. She decided that on her next day off she would ride up to the college and talk to the girls.

She met Amy and Ann after their last class on Thursday afternoon and shared the information. "Girls, I want to tell you about something I found out this week. I went to see the person that is over the lab department at the hospital and told him about our interest in doing DNA testing. You are each over eighteen, so you would not have to have your mother's consent. They would draw a small amount of blood from each of you. It would be sent off, processed, and then they will be able to tell you if you are related at all. There will a percentage to tell you if you come from the same family. Who knows, your great grandfathers could have been brothers, or your grandfathers could have been cousins.

"Now we should not do this without Dottie's permission. But if she will agree, I will pay for the entire procedure. I will be able to get an employee discount. They will not need to test me since we already know that we are not related. That would help a lot on the cost.

"You each need to think very carefully about this. You could talk with Dottie, and she could be upset. Or you could find out that you are not related at all and that it is just a wild coincidence that you two look so much alike. But the most important thing is that you talk to Dottie first. And once you do, and she agrees, contact me, and we will schedule an appointment."

"Mom, you are the best. I really think we are going to be cousins, and then we can finally know our families' history. Maybe our relatives are from Scotland or Ireland or England or who knows where they are from. But we can find out." Amy was filled with excitement.

"Miss Suzanne, I can't thank you enough for going to all this trouble, but I don't know if my mom will agree. I think she must not want me to know anything about her family or my dad's family. There was a problem before I was born, and she won't tell me what it was. All she will say is that she is my family and they are not important. I have always wondered why," Ann said sadly.

"Well, Ann, it is important not to do this behind her back. She would be more upset if we did, and she found out later." Suzanne continued. "So I am going to give you this twenty dollars for you to use for gas.

I want you to go home and talk with her and find out how she feels about it. If she says no, then it will be the end of the story. If she says yes, we will schedule the test for Christmas break. It will take some time to get the results."

"Mom, do you think there is any way that they could go back and find out who my birth parents were even though there were no blood samples left at the wreck?"

"Well, I don't know, but it might connect you with other people in the database, and they may have some information. That really would be a nice thing to find out. You might even have cousins close by," Suzanne said with a smile.

The girls waited for classes to be over Friday. Ann left to go home without her mother knowing she was coming. This was going to be a difficult conversation, and she was not sure how her mother would handle any of it. She was determined to find out the truth now that this door had been opened, and she wanted her mother to finally give her answers to some of the questions she had asked all of her life. She thought about how to approach her mother with this the entire drive home.

'Mom, I am home. I came to see you for the weekend. Mom, where are you?" Ann runs into the den where her mother is usually sitting, but she was not there. Ann went out to the backyard, and her mother was sitting by a fire pit, looking through a folder of papers. "Mom, did you not hear me come up? What are you reading?"

"Ann, I am so glad to see you."

"Mom, why are you crying? What is wrong? What can I do to help?" Ann said reaching over to hug her mom.

"Ann, oh my dear, Ann, I have so much to tell you. I just don't know where to begin or even how to help you understand. But my sweet girl, this is going to be a long night. I have to find a way to tell you the whole story. It may change things forever."

"Mom, what are you saying? Nothing will ever change the love I have for you. Just tell me. You are scaring me and making me really nervous."

"Oh, Ann, where do I start? I just don't know what to say or how you can ever understand. I was a very young woman when I had a miscarriage. When that happened, I did not handle it very well. I could not believe that the baby that I had wanted so badly was gone. My boyfriend and I had planned on getting married. We were going to have a summer wedding, and most of it was planned. But then when I found out I was pregnant, we decided to elope.

"On the night that we were supposed to leave, he called me and told me that he did not want to get married. I did not take the news well. I ran out of the house and got in the car and sped off. I am really not sure what happened after that, but I remember waking up in the hospital, and my baby was gone. I would not believe that my baby was gone and that my boyfriend never wanted to see me again. I had a nervous breakdown and was put in a hospital for a few months.

"When I got out, all I could think about was my baby. She would have been almost a year old, and I wanted to turn back time so I could redo that night."

"Oh, Mom, I am so sorry. Why haven't you ever told me this?" Anne asked.

Dottie clutched something tight in her hand as she tried to continue. "Ann, this is only the beginning. I just pray that you will not hate me. Please let me continue while I have the nerve. It had been about a year and a half since my baby died, and I had just been able to drive again. She would have been almost a year old. I had taken a ride, and I came up on a terrible wreck. The car had exploded, and the people in the car were burnt beyond recognition."

"Oh, *no*, Mom, no." Ann started trembling.

"I heard a baby crying, and while nobody was looking, I picked the baby up and ran to my car. That baby was you. I left you in the car while I went back over and tried to get information. Nobody saw me pick you up. I moved to a new town and dropped all contact with my family. They found me and for a while tried to convince me to come home. I would not. I could not tell them I had stolen a baby."

"Mom, what are you telling me? I am so confused. What do you mean by all of this?"

"Let me continue," Dottie said through her tears. "I have to get this out. I had kidnapped you from the wreck. Nobody knew that you existed. The news was looking for a family of three. The wreck had supposedly just been a couple with one child. That is why nobody ever put things together. I did not know about Amy. All I knew was that you were beautiful, and I had a little girl. You were wearing a necklace with the name Ann on it. So I decided to keep that name," Dottie said as she opened her hand to show the necklace.

"You would be my little girl, Ann. When I moved to a new town with a new baby, I told people that I had lost my husband and that you and I just needed a new start in a new place. People seemed to believe it. I raised you with the idea that one day I would have to tell you the truth. I just wanted it to be when I was so old that you would not leave me. I have been so afraid of someone finding out."

"Mom, this is just too much. How did you do this without ever being caught? How did you keep this from me? Why did you keep this from me?"

"Ann, it was part of my mental state when I had the nervous breakdown. For a long time, I did not remember what I had done. I just remembered that I had a baby. When my counselor was helping me through another difficult time, it all came back. I did not tell him. I just quit going and decided this would have to be my secret. So you can see how it hit me rather hard when you and Amy wanted to do the DNA testing. I knew it would show that I was not your real mother. I did not know what to do. I came home and found the papers I had saved about the wreck. I started reading to see if there was anything that would give me any clarity as to what to say to you. It has not. I just know that I had to tell you even if it means losing you."

"Mom, you won't ever lose me. I am angry and upset, but I will never not love you. But what are we supposed to do about this? What do I tell Amy and Miss Suzanne? How can they possibly understand any of this? How can I ever understand it?"

"Well, I guess the first thing to do is for me to finally go to the police and tell the full story. Then we will call Amy and her mom and tell them to go ahead with the DNA test. I owe you that much. After that, we will see what legal charges will be filed against me. This is not going to be easy. It is going to take a long time. I am actually glad that the truth is out. Maybe now I can finally let go of the guilt I have carried for the past eighteen years. I love you so much, and if you leave now, I will understand. I would not blame you at all."

"I am not going anywhere until all of this is straightened out. I am going to call Amy and talk to her. I think we should at least start there. I am going to go to bed and call her in the morning."

That night, Dottie and Ann did not sleep. Each of them kept thinking of the news that had just been shared, and each one wondered what would happen. The next morning, Dottie walked into the kitchen and found Ann fixing breakfast for her. She could tell that Ann had not slept and looked as if she had cried the entire night.

"Mom, sit down and let me fix you some breakfast."

"Ann, I can't believe you did this for me. I could not sleep, and I know you did not sleep either. We need to decide what we are going to do."

"You are right about what you said last night. We need to go to the police station and talk with someone there. Perhaps they can guide us through this. Let's eat and then we will get ready. If you would like, I could call and see if they would send someone over here."

Ann called the police station and explained the situation. She asked if a police officer would be kind enough not to use the lights and if they could use an unmarked car so the neighbors would not see, she would appreciate it. The police did arrive in an unmarked car within just a few minutes.

Dottie sat with them and explained every detail. She even told them of how difficult it had been keeping this secret for all these years. The police did tell her that they would need to arrest her and that she would face kidnapping charges. Everyone in the town that had known her would be able to testify to the fact that she had been a very good mother and been involved with Ann's life and activities in a positive way.

Ann waited until the police had taken her mother to the police station to call Amy and Suzanne. When Amy answered the phone, she could barely understand Ann because of how hard Ann was crying.

"Amy, this is horrible. You are not going to believe what I have just found out. Amy, we are twins."

"What, what are you talking about? We can't be twins. My parents were killed in a wreck, and I was the only one that survived."

"Well, during the time that the police and fire department were working to put out the car fire and talking to people around them, my mom saw me laying in the grass. She picked me up and put me in her car and pretended I was her baby.

"She had lost a baby the year before and had a nervous breakdown and had been hospitalized for a long time. When she got out, she was driving down the road and came up on the wreck. She saw me and decided to take me. She left her family and moved away and would never tell anyone. When we were at your house for Thanksgiving, she realized she could not handle it any longer without telling me. When I got home last night, she was sitting outside in the cold by a fire pit, looking through papers she had saved of the wreck. She even had a necklace with my name on it just like the one you have. She had kept everything that she could find so that when the time came she could show it to me.

"I had no idea that she was not my mother. Amy, we are twins. I was at that wreck too. The reason the police did not know to look for anyone that had two children was that nobody knew about me. I am so sorry for what she did."

"Ann, the big question right now is are you okay, and is Dottie okay? Are you okay? What can we do to help right now?"

"Amy, I just really wish you were here. I don't know how to handle this."

"Well, consider it done. I will call Mom and she will be here in a few hours and we will be on our way."

After a few hours, Amy and Suzanne had arrived. The three of them went to the police station to talk with Dottie. The lawyer that had been assigned to her would meet them there, and they would figure out what was to happen next. She would go in front of a judge the next morning. Everything was happening so fast, and none of it made sense. But the four of them were now a family, and they would go through this together.

Suzanne was able to fill in some of the facts about the wreck and what the police had tried to do to find the family. No family had ever been discovered. She had no idea if there was anything or anyone that would be available to them now.

The bail hearing was held the next day. She was released and would be standing trial in the next few months for kidnapping. In the meantime, the girls would go through with the DNA test and see if they could find out any additional information.

It took several weeks before they would hear from the test. The lab work came back, and it proved that they were sisters. The lab was also able to trace information to a family that lived in South Carolina. They had a son that had been tested to see if he could find relatives. This son was Eddie. The girls contacted him through an attorney, who let him know that he had been matched with a couple of people who wanted to meet him.

Beth and Charlie were willing to let everyone meet at their house. Beth was rather cautious to make sure that this was not a scam. She had lost her sister and she would not let these people hurt Eddie or her the way that the loss of Nan, Ed, and their nieces had done.

A meeting was scheduled with the attorney to make final plans. The girls, their mothers, and the attorney would travel to a small town in South Carolina. Many of the townspeople had been there when the wreck happened, and they were the ones that knew how hard the family had tried to find out what had happened to their relatives.

When they arrived, the attorney sat down and began to tell the story. The girls were very quiet. The attorney told Eddie and his family that the wreck had been near the mountains of Georgia and that the report had been of a family with one little girl. The little girl had survived and had been placed in a foster home and later adopted. There was no knowledge of a second child. So when reports came through looking for a family in South Carolina, there were no clues. Since the family was to drive straight home, the possibility of them being in Georgia had never been suggested.

The attorney continued to tell of how Ann had been taken from the scene and that nobody had known of her existence. She had been kidnapped by Dottie, who had recently had a miscarriage and had experienced a nervous breakdown. She came up on the wreck and saw a little girl in the grass. She picked her up and put her in her car. The little girl was wearing a necklace with the name Ann on it. Dottie had been a good mother to Ann. She had taken care of her and loved her, and even though she knew what she had done was wrong, she never regretted the love they shared.

Amy had been adopted by Suzanne, the nurse at the wreck, and had also had a very loving relationship with her. They had lived in the same area the entire time, and the people there knew how much Suzanne had done for Amy when she was taken to the hospital and how much she had always loved her.

The attorney continued to tell Eddie that each girl had been loved and cared for their whole lives, and now knowing they were sisters, they wanted to meet their family and to be able to fill in the missing pieces of their lives. They were hoping to get to know Eddie and the rest of the family.

He then told Eddie that nobody knew anything about the circumstances of the wreck. A man had driven by just as the car exploded, and went for help. By the time the fire department and police got there, the car was unrecognizable, and at that time there was no way to get evidence or any information about the people. The fire department had seen the remains of two people in the front seat, but there was no sign of the girls. As you have heard, they were thrown out of the car.

Eddie sat there in disbelief. After all these years, he finally knew what had happened to his parents and his sisters. He was now sitting across the room from them, and they were complete strangers. He had a lot of anger and confusion building up as the attorney continued to tell the story.

Eddie finally spoke. "But why are you together if you did not know of each other until now? Why was I left out? And why weren't they able to find my family when this happened?"

"Well, that is what we are getting to. The girls had not known each other but ended up selecting the same college. They ran into each other at the library and realized they looked alike. They became good friends very quickly. They have spent the first semester at college together and have gotten to know each other. Amy invited Ann and her mom, Dottie, to join them in Georgia for Thanksgiving. Dottie was unsure about going because of the secret she had kept all these years, but she went for Ann. Once there, the possibility of doing the new DNA testing was discussed. That is when Dottie realized her secret had to come out and she had to tell Ann the whole story. That, Eddie, is what has brought us to you and Beth," the attorney continued.

"Well, Dottie should be in jail," Eddie insisted.

"Eddie, no. Don't talk like that," Beth jumped in. "If Dottie had not found Ann and cared for and loved her, we might not be here today. Yes, she did wrong, but she has loved Ann, and we should be thankful for that."

"How can you say that? If they had known that there were two girls and that their names were Amy and Ann, we might have had a chance of finding them."

"Eddie, they were in Georgia. When Ed and Nan left, they were going straight home, which is in the opposite direction. We searched every route in South Carolina. Back then, we did not have the internet to do the searches we can do today. We had no idea they were in Georgia. And we have no idea why they were in Georgia. I can only guess that your mom decided that she wanted to make a detour and do some sightseeing. I am just thankful that the two of them are sitting here with us now. I thought this was going to be a scam but looking at these two is like looking at Nan. They are even wearing the necklaces that Charlie and I gave them the day they were baptized. There is no way that anyone could know about those necklaces," Beth tried to explain.

"Girls, would you each take off your necklaces and turn them over and read to Eddie what is on the back?"

Amy spoke first. "Mine says 'love you. B&C.'"

Ann spoke up. "Mine too. I always wondered who B&C were. It is for Beth and Charlie. Oh my, we had a clue the whole time."

"That is right. Charlie had them engraved when he picked them up from the jewelry store. We had two boys and Eddie but no little girls. We were so excited to have little girls in our family."

"Well, what happens next?" Eddie asked. "I am not sure what I should be feeling right now. Should I call my attorney to get his advice? I mean, I am sure it is all above board, but when you are twenty-six years old and meet your sisters for the first time in eighteen years, you have to make sure you are protected."

Beth was shocked. "Protected from what? What in the world do you need to protect yourself from? Are you worried the girls are here to take your share of our company? No, we do not need protections. What we need is time to get to know each other and to find out as much as we can about what happened that day. I am not sure if there is any way to get any other details but now at least we know where they were. We know what happened to them, and we know that our Amy and Ann are alive and with us now."

"I might have an idea where to start." Dottie quietly spoke. "I kept every article I could find about the wreck. There was one person who came forward and said that a family with two young girls had stopped by the diner she worked in for lunch. She described the two little girls, and they did fit Amy's description. Because there was only one little girl found at the wreck, the information was dismissed. The police in Georgia were looking for information on two adults and a little girl. The police in South Carolina were looking for four people. I never heard anything about the investigation in South Carolina, but the diner is still opened, and it could be that someone there remembers the waitress. We could try."

"Good idea, Mom. We can go by there on our way back to Amy's. There is always a chance." Ann sounded excited.

The attorney felt like it was time to leave, so the family decided that they would get back together in a few weeks and spend some time together. They would try to have other family members present and, of course, Uncle Charlie would be there to greet them.

During those weeks, the attorney, a private investigator, and a police officer that helped at the scene of the wreck worked to dig up evidence. Things had changed a lot since 1968, and perhaps going through the dead files on this case would bring about additional information.

The girls and Suzanne went to the diner. To their surprise, the waitress was now the owner of the diner, and she did remember that day. It seemed as if a lot of people who had gone by the wreck had come in and had told her about it. She had always wondered if it was that family with the twin daughters that had been in earlier that day.

When she saw the girls, she recognized the necklaces. It seemed as if Amy had been chewing on the corner of hers, and the waitress had committed on it. She remembered talking to the couple, and they had told her that they were from South Carolina and were taking a detour home so that they could ride through the mountains. She had never given much thought to it after the investigation of the wreck had settled down. But now eighteen years later, she was looking at those two girls again.

This information would at least tell the family why they had been in Georgia and not in South Carolina. It wasn't going to explain what happened to the car or why it exploded. It did tell them that this was a deliberate trip and that the family had made the decision to go to Georgia.

During this time, Dottie had been at home and was not allowed to travel without the attorney until after the trial. The trial was about to begin. She was not sure what was going to happen or if she would ever see Ann again.

The attorney went to see her the day before the trial with some additional news that she was not expecting. It seemed as though Beth, Charlie, and Eddie were going to be at the trial. They had each requested an opportunity to speak before the trial actually started. The attorney was there to ask her permission. He told her that he had not spoken to Ann about any of this. Dottie felt like she had no other choice but to allow them to speak. She owed them so much more than that. However she was very afraid of what they were going to say and asked the attorney if this could make things even worse for her.

That was far from the truth. Charlie spoke first. He told the judge of how things had been for his family the day Ed, Nan, and the girls were lost to them. He explained how he and his family had accepted Eddie into their home and had raised him as a son and that no matter what the court decided to do, he wanted them to know that Amy and Ann would now be treated the same way, and if they would allow it, Suzanne and Dottie would also be a part of their family.

Beth spoke next. "I was devastated at the thought of losing my sister and her family. I was so grateful that Eddie had stayed with us. He was such a wonderful child and has become a strong, healthy, secure young man. The loss of his family was very hard on him. We did take him to a counselor, and we did walk through the struggles with him. But as his aunt/mom, I could not be prouder of him. Now that we know that Amy and Ann are alive, I think that we deserve a chance to be a family. We want to include Amy, Ann, Suzanne, and Dottie into our family and work through all of this together."

Finally Eddie spoke. "Judge, I don't know much about the law in this area, and I surely do not understand anything that has happened. What I do know is that I have spent eighteen years thinking that my entire family had just disappeared. Now I know what happened, and I know that my sisters are alive. We have lost a lot of time together. I was eight years old when I decided to stay with my aunt and uncle for a few more weeks. If it had not been for that, I would have probably died with my parents. I believe that we deserve a chance to be a family now.

"We do not understand what Dottie was going through when she lost her baby and had a nervous breakdown. We do not know what she was going through the day she kidnapped Ann. But we do know that she has given Ann a life full of love. She has cared for her, provided for her, and loved her as any mother would. I also believe that she has dealt with this in silence for long enough. It is our family's hope and prayer that you will be understanding and allow us to drop all charges of kidnapping. If we are given this gift, I believe that my sisters, their moms, and our family will now be able to be one big family."

Dottie sat on the side of the courtroom in amazement. Suzanne, Amy, and Ann had no idea this was happening, but everyone was in tears and in shock as to the love that this family was able to show Dottie.

The judge called for a recess and told them that he would return after lunch with his decision. The judge and Dottie's attorney met for a couple of hours to discuss every option. This was not a decision to be taken lightly. He could listen to his heart and let Dottie go. He could follow the letter of the law and charge her with kidnapping. Either decision was not going to be popular with some people.

He took a little while to think about it, and then he came back to the court room and called the family back in. He discussed his thoughts with them and asked each girl what they felt about it all. He then talked with Dottie. He gave Dottie a chance to speak with him without anyone around. Then finally he asked everyone to come back into the courtroom.

As they entered, they did not sit down. Dottie was standing by the defense attorney, and the entire family walked up and stood with her. This was highly out of order. The judge did not say anything to them.

He began to speak. "I must say that this is one of the most unusual cases that I have ever heard in my court room. And you, each one of you, is a part of an amazing family. Your support and care for each other is an example to all of us. Let me say that the tragedy that has brought you together is one that I am truly sorry for. You went through a difficult situation that changed the lives of each of you.

"Amy and Ann, you were raised by two loving women, but you lost the opportunity to know your birth family. Beth and Charlie, you lost your family and were suddenly given another son who had questions that you could not answer. Eddie, at the very young age of eight, you had your world turned upside down, and you wanted answers that were not to be found. I cannot imagine how this was for you. Suzanne, I believe we will all agree that Amy was fortunate that you came up on this wreck and that you opened your heart to her.

"And that brings us to Dottie. Dottie, I know that the miscarriage and breakdown that you endured was a part of why you made the decision that you did. You have lived with the guilt and shame of this act for over eighteen years while at the same time giving Ann all the love and care that any mother would do. You have been charged with kidnapping, and this family has asked that the charges be dropped. After hearing from each of you and honestly taking time to pray and ask God for His guidance, I believe that I have come to a decision. It is the decision of this court that Dottie will be charged with kidnapping and will be given probation for a period of one year instead of jail time.

"Dottie, you will need to check in with your probation officer every two weeks, and you will need to ask the court to grant permission before you leave the state. It is my hope that this family will be able to find the answers they need and that you will continue to show the spirit that you have shown in this courtroom. May God bless each of you."

The judge left, and then the family left the courtroom. They all gathered at Suzanne's and spent time making arrangements for a large family vacation where they could continue the journey of getting to know each other. Charlie and Beth would be able to tell the girls about their family and about their heritage. They were now on the way to having the answers they had searched for.

Loral Lake Inn

"Welcome to Loral Lake Inn. May I help you?" As I turned around, I saw a familiar face. "Oh, I never expected to see you here. What brings you back to town?"

"Jane? I can't believe it's you. I am here for Beth's wedding. More importantly, what are you doing here? You are the one who said you would never come back to Rogerston. How did your parents ever convince you to come home?"

"Let's get you checked in. You are in room 10, top of the stairs, last room on the left. I knew your family was going to be here, but I had no idea that you were on the guest list."

"I know where the room is, and I couldn't miss my niece's wedding now, could I?"

"We will catch up later. The life of an innkeeper is very busy."

I walked into the kitchen and sat down at the table. I could not believe that he was here. Not Ken. Of all people, of all times. Why did he have to come to *this* wedding? This was the first wedding near the pier and at the new gazebo. It was also the anniversary of the last time I had seen him.

Ken had been my first love. We had dated all through high school and college. After college, we had come home and planned a future together.

Everything was working out until one day I realized that I had never been on my own. I had never dated anyone else, and I had never lived anywhere but in Rogerston. I wanted to be sure that this was where I wanted to live the rest of my life before following the path that everyone, including Ken, expected me to follow.

One night, I asked Ken to meet me at the pier on Loral Lake. That was the place we spent a lot of time together. It was the place he first told me that he loved me, and it was the place that he had asked me to marry him. I got there before him and tried to rehearse what I would say. I knew that the words would not come out right, but I was trying to let him know that I had to leave to find myself.

"Hi, beautiful. How is the future Mrs. Smith? You look fantastic."

"Hi, Ken. Can we talk for a few minutes?"

"I have never heard that sound in your voice before. What's up?"

"Seriously, I have something that we need to talk about, and I need you to listen."

"Okay, are you telling me you are ready to set our wedding date?"

"Ken, no, I mean it. I have to tell you something. I am not sure that getting married and staying here is what I want to do. We started dating when I was fifteen, and we have never dated anyone else. You were sixteen, and you seemed like, and still are, the perfect person for me. But all through high school and college and even now, we have never been apart. I don't know what is out there for me. I feel like I have to leave Rogerston to find out. Are you willing to leave here and find a life somewhere else? Can you go with me and find out where we should be, what we should be doing? I just don't think Rogerston is where I want to live. Ken, what do you think? Don't just sit there, talk to me. I want you to come with me."

"Wow, I sure was not expecting that. I thought you were ready to buy that little house out in the country and get married and start our own family. You know, the way we had always planned...I guess I was wrong."

That conversation has stayed with me for the past thirty-five years. Ken did not go with me. Instead he called off our engagement. I left town alone. I would come home for visits to see my family, but I never saw Ken. I would hear about him from family and friends, but it seemed as if I would never see him again.

I had gone to Atlanta. I had worked with a company designing and building housing developments and had become very successful. Our communities were based on each house having a front porch and a welcoming entrance. Each neighborhood had a community center that was shared by all the residence. The growing trend for retirement communities had led me to my last job, where we had bought a large tract of land with a lake and created the ultimate retirement community.

My success in my family life had not been quite the same. I had married and had two sons. My children were very small when their father left, and I had raised them on my own. Each of them had become their own person and had a life of his own. I had never remarried and had never been in another serious relationship. I was devoted to my children and my work.

I had been able to live happily in Atlanta until about eight years ago. My father became ill, and my mother needed me to come home and help her with the bed-and-breakfast business they owned. It was a fifteen-bedroom house that had been converted to a bed-and-breakfast when I was a little girl. I spent most of my time by the lake during my youth.

I had taken a leave of absence from my work and had come home to help my parents. My father passed away a few months after I had gotten home.

I decided to stay for a few weeks longer to help my mother adjust to running the business by herself. Those few weeks turned into months and months into years. Each time I thought of leaving, there was a reason for me to stay. I resigned my position in Atlanta and moved home with my mother.

As time passed, I realized that being in Rogerston is where I wanted to be, and I was glad to be home. A few years after my father passed away, my mother died suddenly of a heart attack. I was an only child, so the bed-and-breakfast became mine. I tried to keep it going and had started having weddings and receptions there to bring in some extra income.

I had not known much about what had happened to Ken. I did know that a few years after I left, he met and married someone and that they had two daughters. Ken had stayed in Rogerston for a few years, but he and his family had later moved to Charlotte to be closer to his wife's family. From everything I had heard, Ken had gotten the dream family that he wanted. He was supposedly very happy and a successful real estate attorney.

Ken's sister and I had kept in contact after I returned to Rogerston. We had agreed to never talk about Ken, so she had not told me he would be here for the wedding.

When her daughter asked if she could have the wedding on the pier of Loral Lake, I first said that it was not a good idea. The pier was not big enough for many people to stand. I decided since it was Ken's niece that I would have a huge gazebo built right in front of the pier. It would be the perfect place for an outside wedding. The lake would be a beautiful backdrop. I had the plans drawn up, and construction started before showing them the place. She loved it, and she would be the first bride to have her wedding under the gazebo.

The construction was finished weeks before the wedding. The landscape had been completed, and now it was time for the wedding weekend. The bride and her family had reserved every room in the inn. I had hired extra help for the entire event. Nothing had been said about Ken the entire time they were planning the wedding and reserving rooms or planning the menu. I had assumed that he would not be there.

I knew he had two daughters who would be coming in the day of the wedding. I was nervous about the possibility of meeting them because I had no idea if Ken had ever mentioned that he had a girl-friend when he was younger from his hometown. It would be nice to meet them and see what they were like. I wondered if they had their father's happy-go-lucky disposition. I wonder if their mother was going to be with them. I wondered what she was like.

Sitting in the kitchen remembering all of the past was almost more than I could deal with. I knew I had to get back out there, and I had to give Beth and Johnnie the best wedding that Loral Lakes Inn could provide. After all, she was Ken's niece. I had been there when she was born, and I had always thought she was a special person. I could not let my feelings ruin her big weekend. Ken, or no Ken, this was Beth's weekend. I had to get back out there and quit hiding in my kitchen.

The wedding rehearsal was only a few hours away. The rehearsal dinner was cooked and served to perfection. The music was fantastic, and the entire evening felt like the beginning of a great future for Beth and Johnnie. The weekend was off to great start. If only the rest of the weekend would go like the rehearsal I knew I could get through it.

Beth came to me after the rehearsal dinner to thank me for all that I had done. She knew that seeing Ken was a surprise for me, and she wanted to make sure that I was going to be okay. I told her that my relationship with Ken had been over years ago and that it was fine. We had each moved on so seeing each other again was not a problem. But deep down inside, I knew that it was a huge problem.

After all the guests left, and the kitchen staff had finished, I decided to take a walk. I walked down to the pier. That infamous pier had been my "go-to" place all of my life, and tonight was no different. Seeing Ken had stirred up many emotions, and I wanted to sit on the pier alone, quiet, and away from the inn.

I had been sitting there for about thirty minutes when I heard someone come up behind me. My heart started racing. I turned around, and it was Ken.

"I thought I might find you out here."

"It had been a long day, so I came out to unwind. The rehearsal and dinner went good. Beth is a lovely bride. She has everything so organized and planned out. Tomorrow will be a beautiful day for her. I am sure that she and Johnnie will enjoy every minute of their day."

"Do you remember the last time we were on this pier? It is a night that I have thought of every day for the past thirty-five years. I let you walk out of my life, and I have regretted it ever since. Don't get me wrong, I loved my wife and our two girls, and we had a good life together. My girls are grown and are so much like her. They are happy and fun and full of life. Or like she was. I lost my wife to cancer a couple of years back. I had actually come back to Rogerston to see about opening up a law firm here but found out that you were at the inn, so I decided to stay in Charlotte. I could not bear the idea of you being here and me not being able to see you. I hear you have a family of your own. Two boys?"

"That's right. Tim is in Augusta where he is a golf pro, and Mike is finishing up his last year of school before becoming a veterinarian. They come here from time to time to visit. Tim is married to a wonderful person named Debbie. Mike is engaged to Ann and hopes to be married as soon as he finishes school. Unfortunately things did not work out for their dad and me. We divorced when the boys were young. My work was good though. I helped design and build neighborhoods all around Atlanta. My last job was to build a retirement community. You know, I have thought about a retirement community here that would give people a place on the lake and also give them a place close to town and to a hospital."

"Why don't you? There are lots of people looking for retirement homes, and it does seem to be a great idea for the land. I could help you get started. I am a real estate lawyer you know. I mean, if you would like my help."

"It would cost a great deal of money that I do not have, and I don't have the contacts here that I had in Atlanta. I don't think I can handle something like that on my own. I would need investors and an architect and so much more."

"Well, I am sure your old company still has the house plans, and they may be willing to invest in this project because of the work they know you can do. It would be worth a phone call, don't you think?"

"Oh, that is just a dream. It's like so many other dreams I have had through the years. And dreams need to stay dreams. Ken, have you ever wished things would have been different? Have you ever wondered what would have happened if I had not left Rogerston or if you had come with me?"

"Every day of my life. Like I said, I loved my wife, and we had a wonderful life together. I could not have asked for anyone better to raise our two girls with. We shared a good life and for that I am forever thankful. But there is always something about your first love that you never forget. I tried to keep up with what was going on in your life for a while. I knew you had become a big housing developer. Your company is always in one magazine or another. I did not know about you coming back home, which explains why your name seemed to disappear from all of their published articles. I had wondered if you had quit. Now I know, you returned to the 'land of your youth.'"

"Ken, you could never stay serious. The land of my youth, really, is that how you remember this place? I am surprised that you know about my business. Do you think a retirement community could work on the other side of the lake? I own enough land. I could probably have about a hundred tracts cleared out by the end of the year. The other tracts could be cleared over time. Oh, what am I thinking? I can't do that. It is just a foolish thought. I have to get back to reality. I have a wedding here tomorrow. Are your girls coming in early? Beth did say her cousins were coming. She just forgot the part about her uncle."

"I am supposed to meet them in town tomorrow. We are going to have lunch with my parents at the assisted living home and then come back out here for the wedding. I had tried to get them to stay a few days, but they are each so busy with their own lives. And since their mom died, it is hard for us all to be together."

"I hope I get a chance to see them. Maybe I can tell them what their dad was really like when he was in high school."

"Why would you do that? I don't want them to think they can get by with things just because their old man did. Besides, they would never believe you."

"I need to head back to the house and start getting things together for tomorrow. Enjoy the rest of your evening."

I went back up to the inn and started setting up the tables for the reception and making sure everything was in place. Everyone else had already gone to their rooms except Beth. She was sitting on the sofa in front of the fireplace.

"Beth, are you okay? Shouldn't you be getting some rest?"

"Miss Jane, I have always heard the story about how my Uncle Ken loved you so much and y'all were going to get married, but you decided you wanted to leave Rogerston. I saw the two of you talking, and I can't help but see how he looked at you. He never looked at my aunt that way. What if I am like you and I don't want to live here? What if I want to move away? It's too late to say anything to Johnnie. I don't know why I am thinking like this tonight. Tonight of all nights. This is the night before my wedding, and I have the most wonderful man in the world upstairs waiting to become my husband. What is wrong with me?"

"Oh, Beth, nothing is wrong with you. You are just nervous about the wedding. You love Johnnie, and Johnnie loves you. That is enough to get through anything. You are right. Your Uncle Ken and I did have a very special relationship. He was the best thing that had ever happened to me except the birth of my two boys. I loved him in a way that I could never have loved anyone else. But the truth is, I was too young to realize what I wanted. It had all been planned out for me, and it seemed as if nobody had thought about what I wanted to do. I got scared, and I ran. That was the biggest mistake of my life. You will be just fine. You need to go upstairs and get a good night sleep and think about what a wonderful day tomorrow will be when you walk down that aisle and marry the man of your dreams. That is what Johnnie is. I can see it when you are together. Trust me when I say that tomorrow will be a wonderful day."

"Goodnight, Jane. You are right. Johnnie and I do belong together, and if it means staying here, then we stay here. Who knows, we might get to move to some other place like Uncle Ken and you did."

"Goodnight."

Everyone had come in for the night except Ken. I looked out the door as I started locking up and saw that he was still sitting on the pier. I walked back down there and asked him if he was okay.

He looked at me and nodded. I saw a tear in his eye. I wasn't quite sure what to do so I just sat down beside him and held his hand. He squeezed my hand and put his head on my shoulder.

"Ken, do you want to talk?"

"No, not really. Just being here makes me regret so many things. I have to still be that happy-go-lucky guy around the family, but sometimes being alone and thinking of my past makes me very sad. I don't know why my wife had to get cancer, and I don't know why she had to leave us at such an early age. I do know that she loved my girls, and my girls loved her. I just feel so lonely."

"I can understand that. I felt that way for many years after my husband left. Events like tonight where everyone has a partner but me always make me feel like I do not fit in anymore, even at family events. It is hard to be alone. Occasions like this make it even harder. Let's get back to the inn, and I will fix you a cup of coffee."

"It is getting very late. We should go inside."

Ken took my hand, and we walked back to the inn. We sat in front of the fireplace for a while, and he told me all about his wife and daughters. He told me about his work as an attorney and how he had his real estate license and that is what he really enjoyed doing, but there was not enough money in it, so he only sold houses in his spare time.

He talked for a while and then sat back in the chair and fell asleep. I got a blanket and put over him and went to bed. I had so many mixed feelings being around him that I did not know what I was feeling, much less what he was feeling. But tomorrow was Beth's day, and I had to get some sleep and get an early start getting things ready.

The sun was rising and the birds were chirping and that told me that it was time for the day to begin. The kitchen staff had arrived, and a special breakfast was served for everyone but Beth and Johnnie. They were each being served breakfast in their rooms. The tradition of the groom not seeing the bride before the wedding was going to continue at the inn. Ken ate his breakfast and then left to meet his girls and go to his parents'.

Beth's bridesmaids, mother, and Johnnie's mother all headed off to have their hair and makeup done. The fathers and groomsmen sat around as if there was nothing special about the day. Johnnie came down to join them. They turned the television on and watched a ballgame.

Someone realized what time it was, and all of them quickly headed up to their rooms to get dressed. They had to be at the gazebo for pictures before the wedding. They got dressed and came back downstairs. Each one of them was as handsome as the next, and each one was ready to get this wedding going.

The pictures of the groomsmen and the fathers were taken, and everyone got back inside as the bridesmaids came back from getting their hair and makeup done. They headed to the gazebo for their pictures. Everything was going as planned. Just as Beth had done with everything else, she had planned the timing of the pictures just right.

After the pictures were taken and all the girls were back inside, the guests began to arrive. I saw Ken's car driving up. I looked to get a glimpse of his daughters. One of them saw me looking. She walked over to me. "You must be the famous Jane we have heard so much about all our lives. Dad didn't know before he came if you would be here. We had hoped that we would get a chance to meet you."

"I am Jane. I am not so sure what your father has told you about me, but I would like to know if you want to share."

"Not now, girls." Ken spoke up. "We have a wedding to get to. Let's go see Beth get married."

The wedding was absolutely breathtaking. The sun going down over the lake as we danced at the reception made it a picture-perfect wedding. Beth and Johnnie were as happy as any two people I had ever seen. The guests had a great time. But unfortunately all good things must come to an end.

The bride and groom left on their way to their honeymoon, and the guests all went home. There were just a few people that were staying one more night. Ken and his sister and her family were staying as well as his two daughters. He had talked them into staying for the night. They would leave the next morning to head back to their jobs.

Ken asked me to join them as they all reminisced about growing up in Rogerston. I could see how the girls listened as their dad and aunt talked. They made it seem like a fairytale town. I had to admit that was not the way I had seen it growing up, but after coming back and living here for the last few years, it was what I saw now.

Ken told stories of his high school football and basketball days and of my days as a cheerleader. Yes, he did have to take us down memory lane. That night was one of the happiest I had felt in a long time. It was as if time had stood still.

The next morning, everyone came to breakfast and said their goodbyes as they went their different ways. I noticed that Ken was lingering and was in no hurry to leave. He said he wanted to talk with me before leaving. He asked if I would take a walk with him.

We walked out to the gazebo and sat down. He pointed across the lake. "What do you see?"

"I see a beautiful landscape."

"What would you like to see?"

"A beautiful landscape with house spread out around the lake."

"Then that is what we should do. We should build Loral Lake's Retirement Community."

"Ken, that is just a dream. It is just a thought I had. I can't do that."

"You can't. But we can. You own the land. I have money put aside from my wife's insurance, and I had not done anything with it. I can invest it in this plan. We can have the land surveyed and divided into lots. For each lot we sell, we will each take a fourth until my money is paid back. The other half will be used to start the development. With the plans used from your last retirement home development and with an investment from your old company, we could have this development up and going within a year. Of course, you will have to be able to work closely with me. I have my real estate license, and I am a real estate attorney. You have the knowledge to bring this all together. What do you think?"

"First, you are crazy. Second, I think it seems like a dream, and third, we don't have the plans or backing from my old company."

"What if I said we did? I made a couple of phone calls early this morning and told your former partner what I had in mind. He is getting the plans together, and he and an associate will be out here this week to see the land and to talk to us about it. So you see it could work."

"You are amazing. I cannot believe that you did all that early this morning and got me to believe it could happen. I am not sure, but I am willing to talk with them and see what they think. But what about you? I thought you were leaving today."

"I called my office and told them that I would not be in until next week. I had my secretary clear my calendar and change my appointments. The ones she could not change will just see one of the other lawyers in the office. I am here for the week. So what do you say? Do you want to take a boat ride to the other side of the lake, or do you want me to drive my car? It's your choice."

"Well then, let's get the boat ready. Let me go upstairs and change clothes, and I will be right back down. I cannot believe you have talked me into going over there."

I called my sons after we got back from looking over the land. I explained to them this crazy idea and asked what they thought. After all, that land would have been theirs one day, and they may not want me to sell it.

To my surprise, Ken had already reached out to them and told them who he was and that he was going to have each of them a ticket waiting at the airport for them to join us when we met with my former business associates. Each one of them had been a little confused by all of it at first, but as Ken told them the story, they were on board, and each one had already been making plans to be here. It looked as if everything was being taken care of for me. I was not sure how I felt about that, but today it was okay.

The next few days, Ken and I worked through the ideas we wanted to present to my former associates. My sons arrived on Wednesday, and we went over the plans with them. We went over to the other side of the lake and showed them the area of land that we wanted to build the retirement center. I pulled out a sketch that I had been working on and showed them how I saw the land around the lake being developed. Each house would have a view of the lake. The land directly in front of the inn would not be cleared so that the view from our side of the lake would remain much like it was now. We were all in agreement as to what we would present.

On Thursday morning, my former associates arrived at Loral Lake Inn. It was so good to see them, but I did want to keep my mind on business and not let myself fall back into the work mindset we had while working together. He had the plans with him. Ken had our business plan with him. I presented the idea for the retirement home, and we took them to see the land.

Once we got back to the inn, we knew that we had an agreement. It seemed perfect for everyone involved. Within a few months, the land was surveyed, and the lots marked off. We had an office in town for people to come by and see the plans.

Tim and his family would move back to Rogerston, and he would run the office. We made sure to add a golf course to the retirement community, and Tim would run that as soon as it was up and going. His wife, Debbie, would continue to run the business office.

Ken made plans to move back to Rogerston. He would have his law office and real estate office in the office too. I would continue to run Loral Lake Inn.

Everything was in place, and the work was started. We began construction on our first house. This house would be used as a spec house as far as everyone knew. Once the first ten houses and the community center were built, we held a grand opening. The first house that had been built was to be a highlight of the grand opening. Ken gave a speech and thanked everyone for coming. He told everyone of how this had been a dream come true in many ways. It had brought him back to his hometown and had also helped to bring someone very special back into his life.

As he continued to talk, he asked his parents to come forward. They were somewhat caught off guard but did as he asked. I stepped forward and stood beside him. I handed each of them a set of keys and told them that they had always been a major part of my life and were Ken's parents so we felt that it was only right that they be given the keys to the first house in Loral Lake Retirement Community. They were shocked and thanked us and were even more surprised when they opened the door and found many of their things had already been delivered to their new home.

Ken and I continued to work on the development over the next few years. We managed to have one hundred houses with views of the lake and another hundred within walking distance or either a short golf cart ride to the lake.

Ken's real estate business flourished as did his law practice. Tim became the golf pro at the new golf course, and his wife remained as the office manager. One of Ken's daughters joined us as the accountant for the retirement community, and his other daughter would be the nurse at the health clinic after graduation. My other son and his girlfriend moved to Rogerston and opened up an animal clinic. The life that I had walked away from was the life that I now cherished.

Two years after Beth and Johnnie's wedding, Ken and I were married. We continue to live at the inn and continue to dream of our next phase of life. We have completed seventy-five of the homes at Loral Lake Retirement Center and have ten others under construction. We have a long waiting list of people who are wanting to build as soon as our builders are available. Ken has shown me that even when we walk away from our dreams, that if they were supposed to be, somehow, they will come back to us.

Home for the Holidays at Loral Lake Inn

"Ken, can you help me get the Christmas trees out of storage today?" I asked quietly, "It's the end of October, and I have a lot to get done."

"It's October!" Ken explained. "Why are we getting the trees down now?"

"Well," I continued, "it is October, and I have fifteen trees to get up and decorated before Thanksgiving. I need to get each tree set up in the rooms and the boxes of decorations for that tree emptied out, and I need to go through each box. I don't know what else I might need this year. We don't have anyone coming in for several of the rooms between now and Thanksgiving, so I thought it would be a good chance to get started."

"Well, I guess I did sign up for this 'Honey, Do List. Just did not know it would involve all of your Christmas decorations."

"You will see. It will be great."

Each year we decorated the inn. Each room had its own theme. The shared rooms of the inn like the living room, dining room, family room, and kitchen all worked together to bring the house to its best. This year would be different. Ken and I were married. Tim and Mike and their families were living in Rogerston, and Ken's oldest daughter Laura and her fiancé Bill had decided to move here to help run the restaurant we were building at Loral Lake Retirement Center. She had stayed on as an accountant once the Retirement Community had gotten started. Ken's younger daughter, Jennifer would be here the week of Christmas. The hospital where she was a nurse kept her busy, so she did not get home often. We had heard through the grapevine that she was bringing a surprise guest with her.

This would be the first time since Ken and I were married that the entire family would be together. I was excited and nervous to see how this long weekend would go. Tim and Mike had their own homes within just a few miles from the inn. Ken's parents were across the lake in the Retirement Community. The girls and their guest would be staying at the Inn.

It may only be October, but I only had four weeks to get things just right. The gazebo, pier, and front porch would be decorated last. But they had to be finished by the first weekend in December because the town had planned a big event to be held at the gazebo. This was my favorite time of the year, and this year was going to be the best year ever.

Ken did get the decoration down from the storage building, and he put the appropriate tree and box of decorations in the rooms that were not going to be used. I started out by spreading the ornaments out on the beds. I checked each one to make sure that it was still perfect. Each room had to be just right. There were fifteen bedrooms. Ten would be available for guest this year. If I did a tree every few days, I could have it done. And because I loved to plan, I decided to sit down and get organized.

Debbie, Tim's wife had offered to help and so had Mike's fiancé, Ann. She had hinted at wanting to have a Christmas wedding. I was not sure if I should say anything to her, but as long as we were decorating, I thought I would bring it up.

During the next few days, the plans were complete, the menus for Thanksgiving and Christmas were finalized, and the decorations started bringing Christmas to the inn. Each day for the next ten days, we got together and worked on one of the ten bedrooms. They each added to the beauty of the inn at Christmas. We would finish the trees and other decorations for the rooms and shut the doors as if to say this room is ready.

After completing those rooms, we turned our thoughts to the gazebo and pier. I wanted to make that area special for the town event. We decided to get a twelve-foot tree and decorate it with things that would represent the true meaning of Christmas. We would do our version of the Chrismon Tree.

Chrismons are decorations that tell the story of the birth of Christ. Each ornament is white-and-gold, and each ornament is to be handmade. Since we were going to have a large twelve-foot tree, we decided to invite the people from the local churches to donate ornaments. It would sit in the gazebo for everyone to enjoy. We contacted the local churches, and before we knew it, we had box loads of decorations. Not only could we decorate the gazebo, the pier could have its own Chrismon tree.

About two weeks into the decorating, Ken came to me. "Jane, you are doing a great job. I just have one suggestion that I would like to mention. What if I found a sleigh and a horse that we could rent for a few days and offer people rides around the property the night of the town Christmas tree lighting and caroling? What do you think?"

"I think it is a great idea. I know a man in Ward County that has an old sleigh. I tried to get it from him to use as a decoration for in front of the inn. He was not ready to sell it, but he might let us rent it. I can get his name and number for you. I knew that somehow the Christmas spirit would get through to you."

Ken contacted Mr. Matthews from Ward County, and he was willing to rent us the horse and carriage for the day. Not only was he willing to rent it, he was willing to drive the carriage for the rides around the inn. We were even more surprised when he said that he would not charge us rent if we would let him be a part of the town event. He had been given the carriage by his father when his mother passed away. His parents had given rides around the park each Christmas when he was a small boy, and this would be something that would bring memories back for him.

October was gone, and the first three weeks of November were quickly passing. We only had one week before the family would be home, and we only had one more week before our first Christmas guest would arrive. The plans were to have a large Thanksgiving feast for our family and guests. The afternoon would be family time, and the evening would of course be a time for football and Hallmark movies.

The Friday after Thanksgiving had always been a time for us to spend time doing something as a family. I was not sure what that was going to be since our family had grown so much over the past few years. I had no idea that Ken had been planning a big surprise for all of us.

The day before Thanksgiving, our guests arrived. Each room was ready, and each guest was given a basket of goodies to enjoy. The weekend was off to a good start. Thanksgiving morning was filled with cooking and baking, and the kitchen was seeing so much activity that I wondered if there would be a clean dish in the house when we were ready to eat. It was the start of the best holiday ever.

When we all sat down, Ken said grace. After that, he asked us if we would go around the table and say one thing that we were thankful for. Tim was sitting next to Ken, so he started.

Tim started. "I am thankful for each of you and for the success of Loral Lake Retirement Community. I could not ask for a better family."

Debbie said, "I am thankful that each of you has welcomed me into this family and am thankful for my first holiday at the Inn."

Jennifer said, "I am thankful for a week off to be here with my new family and to let each of you get to know someone very special to me."

Ken said, "Speaking of which, where is this person we are supposed to meet?"

Jennifer continued, "He is almost here. I told him that we would save him a plate. His plane was delayed because of bad weather. He should be walking in at any time. And Dad, you had better be nice to Adam. He is really a good guy."

Laura said, "I am thankful that we are here as a family and that the food is finally cooked."

Laura's fiancée, Bill, spoke up. "I have never met a family that was this happy and calm at Thanksgiving. I am thankful for the stress-free day.

It was my turn. "I am thankful for life and love and for the people at this table. Being part of this group is the best."

Mike began. "I am thankful for the people at this table. I am thankful for my mother and brother who have shared my life with me and for Ken, Laura, and Jennifer for making our family complete. I am thankful for my extended family too. But most of all, I am thankful for Ann. I know that we have the rest of our lives to be together, but if it is okay with you, Ken and Mom, we would like to start our married life here at the Inn."

Ann interrupted, "Jane, you know how much I love Mike, and you know that I love this place. I know that this is a very busy time for you, but we were wondering if my parents and sister could join us and perhaps we could have a wedding at the gazebo next weekend. We could have the wedding right before people come for the town tree lighting. I can't think of a better time to be married. Jane, do you think we could make this happen?"

"Are you kidding? I have been waiting for you to ask. I have all the decorations we will need, and if the weather is bad, we can come inside and use the great room and dining room. It will be great. First, let's call your mother and talk to her and see what she thinks. Then we will get started on putting things together. Jennifer, Laura, and Debbie can help, and we will have it done in no time."

"Speaking of them, my sister is going to be my maid of honor. Laura, Jennifer, will you be my bridesmaids, and Debbie, will you be my matron of honor? I know it is short notice, but really it won't matter what you wear."

Debbie spoke up. "I would be honored. I have always wanted a sister. I bet if we get up tomorrow morning and drive to the mall we could find dresses for all of us. Do you have a dress?"

"I do. I bought it a few weeks ago when Mike and I started talking about doing this. We just did not want a big wedding or anyone fussing over us, so we have made most of the plans already. We have the music lined up, the caterer is doing the cake, the florist is doing the bridesmaids' flowers, and we have already talked to the minister. So really, I don't think that there is much planning to do. Jane, are you sure the first Saturday in December is not too much for you? I mean, the town's Christmas tree lighting and all?"

"No, it will make that night even more special. If we have the wedding about two, then we will be done by the time the people get here to set up. It will be the perfect way to start the Christmas holiday.

"Ken," Mike said, "We did not hear what you are thankful for."

"Well, first I am thankful that I don't have to get everything set up for your big day. Secondly, I am thankful for this family and for the love that is in this room. Most importantly, I am thankful that Jane came back into my life and that we are able to be together for the rest of our lives. Now, let's eat."

We all talked about the wedding and the tree lighting during the rest of the meal. After eating, we went around to the tables where our guests were sitting and thanked each of them for being a part of our Thanksgiving, and then the entire family went into the family room and watched television and worked on more plans for the wedding.

The next day, the girls and I got into my van and drove to the nearby mall. We went into the bridal store and found the perfect dresses for each of the girls. Debbie and her sister were the same size, so we got Debbie to try one on, and we got her sister's dress too. They were all set. The girls helped me pick out a dress as mother of the groom.

We went by the caterers and did the final okay for the cake. We went by the florist and put down the deposit for the flowers. The day could not have gone any better. The best part of it all was that we were back home by three in the afternoon. We sat around and watched a couple of Hallmark movies while the guys watched more football.

Ann called her mother, and we all talked about the wedding. She would come up a few days early to help us get ready, and Ann's sister and father would drive up the Thursday night before.

Yes, this Thanksgiving was one that we had much to be thankful for.

That night, when it was almost dark, Ken came into the room and asked us to join him outside. We all went out, and you could see a fire going close to the pier. He had a fire pit built and had chairs set up all around the fire. There was music playing.

As we got closer, I saw two old guitars sitting by the fire. I was not sure, but they did look very familiar. Yes, it was. Those were the guitars that Ken and his good friend played when we were in high school. But why were both of them there?

Ken asked me to turn around and look toward the driveway. I could not believe it. Our dear friend who had been fighting cancer was standing in the driveway. He was home, and he was going to be staying with us. He was celebrating beating cancer the best way he knew. He had come home, and he was going to see all of his old friends and family.

We sat around the fire and listened to them play music and sing and catch up on old times. Ken's girls did not know that he played as well as he did, so they got a special kick out of seeing their dad play and hearing him sing.

After a few hours, we all went back up to the inn, and each went to our own rooms. Ken and I were sitting on our balcony talking about how blessed we really were when there was a knock on the door.

It was Ann's mother. She had gotten things together and decided to come on up. She would be staying with Ann but just had to come by and see us before she went to their house. She loved the inn and the plans that Ann had shared with her.

The plans for the town's event were all complete, and the decorations for the inn were up. The wedding was just a few days away. We were about to have our third family wedding at the gazebo. First

Beth and Johnnie, then Ken and me, and now Mike and Ann.

We all worked to prepare for our big day— Mike and Ann's wedding, the carriage rides, and of course, the tree lighting and caroling. The weather was wonderful the entire week. We were able to have everything in place ahead of schedule.

Mr. Matthews came very early the day of the wedding. He had heard that we were having a wedding and wondered if he could give the bride and her father a lift to the gazebo in his carriage. That was the finishing touch. It was perfect.

The girls were dressed in burgundy winter dresses. The men wore dark grey suits. To everyone's surprise, Ken and his friend sang a special song for Mike and Ann. The wedding and the reception were over by four o'clock. Even the kitchen was cleaned and ready for the next big event.

The people from town came and did their last-minute setup. We watched as people began to fill the driveway. At six o'clock, we walked down to the gazebo to join the crowd. The ministers for several of the churches spoke. Children's choirs sang, and then the tree lights were turned out. It was spectacular.

As the lights on the tree came on, so did the lights all up and down the pier. Carols were being sung, some people were taking sleigh rides around the property, and to end the event, the mayor read the Christmas story from Luke 2. We closed with one last song.

People began to leave, and soon the only people left were the people staying at the inn and our family. Ken and I lingered behind at the pier. We spent a while talking about what a great holiday it had already been.

As we sat there, we noticed that it was getting a little too cold to stay out any longer, so we went back to the Inn.

The next few weeks were very routine. We had the inn to ourselves most of the week but had guests each weekend. It was Christmas week. The snow had started to fall, and the roads were a little icy. We had suggested that Ken's parents come spend Christmas Eve at the inn with us just in case the weather got too bad for them to drive around the lake. All four of the children and their spouses or guests would be staying with us Christmas Eve as well.

We were all dressed and ready to go to Christmas Eve service when we heard a knock at the door. It was Mr. Matthews. He had brought the carriage and was there to take us on a carriage ride to church.

This time, he had a different carriage that was large enough for our entire family.

The church was only a couple of miles from the inn. We all got into the carriage and wrapped up in the blankets and sang carols as we enjoyed our ride to the church. Mr. Matthews went inside with us and sat with our family during the service. Afterwards he drove us home. The weather was beginning to get worse, so we convinced him to spend the night.

The old saying about the inn being full was true that night. There was not an empty room available. It was just the way I had always wanted it at Christmas.

Everyone was settling in and enjoying some nighttime snacks and spiced tea. Ken had a fire going in the fireplace, and all the Christmas lights were on. Even the outside lights were still going. It was Christmas Eve, and this inn was full of activity. Everyone was in place and accounted for. Then suddenly we heard a knock at the door.

Someone was knocking hard, so Ken went to see who was there. It was a young man who apparently had been walking through the snow following the lights to find help for his family. They had run off the road and landed in a ditch. He could not get the car out, so he had decided to try to find help. The lights from the inn were bright enough to show him the way. His wife and two children were waiting in the car.

Ken went out and got the tractor out of the barn. Mike and Tim went with him. The rest of us stayed at the inn and started to get things ready for four more people. We were not sure where we would find room, but there was always room for one more.

One of the families staying with us had gotten two rooms. One room for the couple, and another room for their two daughters. They offered to give up one of those rooms. We gratefully accepted the offer and began to get that room ready. We brought in air mattresses for the children. The room was ready by the time Ken and the others pulled the car into the drive.

The family came in and warmed by the fire. The children looked around at all the decorations. They had never seen so many decorations, and they had never seen such a big house. It was amazing to see the inn through the eyes of small children.

The inn was overflowing with people. It was Christmas Eve. *Oh*, no. It was Christmas Eve. Tomorrow would be Christmas Day. There was enough food for the people we had planned on, but now we had so many more. I needed to get up early and get things started. Who knows what tomorrow would bring?

After all of our guests and family had gone to their rooms, Ken and I went out to the porch and looked out at the gazebo and pier. The pier was as beautiful as I had ever seen it. The snow was falling, and the Christmas lights were shining. We sat on the porch and talked for a few minutes as we finished our tea.

"Jane, thank you for being such a wonderful host. We have my parents, Mr. Matthews, the family that got stranded, and all of the guests you were not expecting. You seemed to be happier with each one that came through the door."

"I am. It was many years ago that an inn became an important part of a story. Just as many of us don't have room in our hearts for Christ, the inn did not have room for Joseph and Mary the night Jesus was to be born. But the innkeeper found room. It may not have been the best room. In fact, it may have not been a place for humans at all. But it was the perfect room for Jesus to be born. I always think about the old saying, 'There is no more room at the inn when our rooms are booked.' It makes me think that there is always room for one more. One more person is always welcomed. Christmas is a reminder of that story. So this year as our inn is full, and all of our family is together, I am very happy."

"Well, it is getting late, and we have a very busy day ahead of us. We need to get in."

"Ken, Merry Christmas. I hope that every person in the inn will feel the true meaning of Christmas and that the celebration of Christ's birth will continue at our inn for many years to come just as it has this year. Thank you for all that you do."

"Merry Christmas to you, Jane."

Merry Christmas to everyone.

Town Picnic at Loral Lake

The cold of winter seemed behind us and the feeling of spring was in the air. Loral Inn had experienced the rooms being booked almost every weekend. The retirement community had been completed, and most of the houses had been sold. Everything was going much better than we could have dreamed with our adventures with Loral Lake. We could not be happier with the decisions to expand and develop the other side of the lake.

"Jane, don't forget we have the city council meeting tonight at seven. Are you going to be able to go with me?" Ken asked.

"Sure, I have heard that they are going to start the plans for the seventy-fifth town picnic. I can't wait to see what they have planned for this year," I answered. "I am interested in seeing how they react to our offer of using the entrance to the lake."

The town council meeting started with regular business, and as planned, the last item on the agenda was this year's picnic. Rogerston had come to be known for the fantastic weekend long event that brought in people from all of the surrounding areas. Games, activities, music, dances and, of course, lots of foods to try were always a big part of the picnic. The weekend would begin with a parade featuring floats from many of the local businesses, churches, and the local high schools' bands. The parade would end with a firework display that was like no other. Following the fireworks, there would be a live band until 11:00 p.m.

The next morning, there would be a car show, a craft show, and vendors selling their goods, and of course, food trucks will be set up all over the fair grounds. Saturday night, there would be live music and dancing until midnight. To finish out the weekend, a town-wide church service will be held with representatives from several of the churches participating in the program. It had been the same thing every year, and this year was looking like there would be a big crowd to plan for.

"Jane," Mayor Smith spoke up, "we have been discussing making some changes to this year's event, and before you say no, we were wondering how you and Ken would feel about having this year's picnic at the entrance to the Retirement Community. It was a great place for our Christmas program. The town will take care of all of the setup and tear down of any equipment used. We would like for y'all to talk this over with your family and let us know."

Ken answered, "That won't be necessary. We have already discussed it with our family, and we were going to make the offer to have everything at

Loral Lake. Not only will this give the people a great location for everything to be in one place, we have the lake for people to enjoy. So we can give you our answer now. Yes, we'd be honored."

"Wow," Mayor Smith said. "We had a list of reasons it would be good to have the picnic there. We were ready to go through the list. If you two are on board, I think we should get busy planning."

"This is not part of the picnic planning," Jason said, "but have any of you noticed a couple of men wondering around the town the last few days? I see these two everywhere I go. If I did not know better, I would think they were sizing our small town up for some reason."

"Yes, they came into the diner last night. I could not hear what they were saying, but they were talking about the town and what is available here. I overheard them talking about the lake and spending time there," Linda remarked. "That made me wonder if one of them had been here before."

Chief Atkins spoke up. "Do you know where they are staying? Jane, Ken, are they staying at the inn? I will try to check in to this. Sounds like we have strangers in town who are snooping around."

Mayor Smith said, "Chief, that won't be necessary. They are our guests. They may have spent time here before and wanted to come back and visit. Let's get back to the picnic planning."

The committee finished up for the night knowing that they only had a few months to pull off the biggest and best picnic ever. Each person was assigned responsibilities and would need to report back to the council at the next meeting.

The roads and grounds at the inn had been redone for the Christmas program so there would not be a big cost there. The lake's boat landing and restaurant were now open and ready for visitors. The traffic would not affect Loral Lake Inn as people were coming and going. Ken had already started building a large portable stage area that could be used for any event but taken apart and stored when not in use. Ken and I were feeling good about the picnic.

Over the next two weeks, there were a number of stories about two strangers walking around town and going to the library to look through old newspapers. They seemed very private and were not reaching out to talk or get to know the people in town.

"Jane, how would you like to go to dinner before the meeting tonight? If we leave early, we can go by the diner and maybe get a look at these two strangers who are in there every night. I just wonder if anyone has taken the time to speak to them. Maybe they are just trying to have a quiet get a way."

"Sure, I can be ready by six, and I really would like to get a double cheeseburger and half-and-half from the diner. Remember every week after school, we would go by the diner and get a half-and-half?"

"I sure do. Sounds like a good choice. I will join you or maybe I will get one of their famous chili burgers."

Ken and Jane finished work for the day and got all of the information they needed for the meeting and headed to the diner. They spoke to Linda as they walked in and noticed the booth they normally sat in was not available. They walked past the two people sitting there, spoke a friendly hello, and sat down at the table next to them.

"Hello, I am Ken, and this is my wife, Jane. Are you visiting our town?" Ken asked.

"We are." One of the men spoke up. "We used to come here to see our grandmother when we were young. We would always go to this place right out of town where the kids played in the lake every day. I met a few friends there, and we stayed in touch for a long time. I never came back to Rogerston after my grandmother passed away. My life went on, and I never knew what had happened to the friends I met here. By the way, I am Tom, and this is my brother, Tim."

"We are glad you came back to visit. Where are you staying?" Jane asked.

"We are staying at our grandmother's house. The house has been rented for many years by the Jones family. Mr. Jones passed away last year, and Mrs. Jones has decided to move to a retirement home right outside the city limits. Perhaps you have heard of it, Loral Lake Retirement Center? We rode past it, and it looks like a nice place," Tom said.

"Well, it just so happens that I know the place. We own it. It has been in my family for years. Once Ken and I decided that we would have a future together, we decided to expand the development. As a matter of fact, Ken's parents were the first people to move in. Our children work with Loral Lake. So it is truly a family place for us," Jane proudly said. "Do you mind me asking who your grandmother was?"

"Her name was Ruth Stanley. She was married to John Stanley. They lived in Rogerston after my mother married, and so it was the place we came to see our grandparents. Our grandfather died very young. My grandmother never remarried but always wanted to keep her house in the family." Tim spoke up.

"Well, Tim, I think I might remember her. Are you talking about the house on the corner of Orr Street and Marion Street? I remember going over there when her grandchildren would come. My mother took me there to play with a young girl. Was she your sister or cousin?" Jane continued.

"That would be Sallie. She is our older sister. She is living in North Carolina now and has not been to the house since the renters moved out. They lived here for more than thirty years. I guess we should think of selling it, but first we needed to find out what it was like and if it needs a lot of work," Tom said.

"We are waiting on Sallie to get here next week. Until then, we have been doing minor repairs and looking up family information at the library. The three of us are going to look through the house and finally open the door to the storage room in the attic that nobody was allowed to open. We have no idea why or what could have been so important, but we are all three going to be there to see it at the same time," Tim said.

Ken said, "Well, just be careful. If the room has not been opened in fifty or more years, there is no telling what could be in there. I think I would have a clear path to run just in case little critters come out when you open the door."

Tom laughed. "Don't think we have not thought of that. I, for one, am not a big fan of rodents of any kind."

"Tom, Tim, it has been nice talking with you. You have solved the mystery of who the two strangers in town are. You are welcome to come out to the inn and visit while you are here. And if you are around when we have the town picnic, please join us," Jane said.

When Ken and Jane shared the information about the two strangers at the council meeting, it seemed as if several of them remembered the children. They said they would make a special effort to reach out to them and make them feel welcome. Jane also shared with them that the granddaughter would be coming and that the three of them were going to be cleaning out the house.

After meeting Ken and Jane, people in town were more open to the strangers and their curiosity about Rogerston. They continued to find out things about their grandparents and other family members by searching old newspapers at the library.

Their great grandfather had served as mayor of Rogerston and had built the house they were about to sell. He had been the one to bring in industries to the area. During his leadership, the town grew to be one of the most successful towns in the area. Newspapers show that their great grandfather suddenly died and that the work that he had started was continued with the next mayor.

Unfortunately there seemed to be a little suspicion around him. He seemed to be a very quiet and private man when he was not at his office. You would often see him go into his house. The only light that would be on late at night was coming through a third-floor window. Nobody in town had ever seen that room. Tim and Tom felt that the locked room held the story to all the mystery surrounding their family. But what was it?

When Sallie arrived, she met many of the people at the diner. It seemed to her that this small town held fond memories of time spent with their grandmother. She did not remember her grandmother ever talking about her father, their great grandfather, or the mayor. It was now time to discover what was in the room.

They did not have a key, so they decided to have someone take the door down so it could be replaced. As the door was opened, it finally told the story—or perhaps the beginning of the story.

They saw beautiful antique furniture with absolutely no dust to be seen. They saw papers stacked on a desk as if they had just been placed there. They saw a room as if it was being used every day and not a room that had been closed for years. They quickly took pictures of everything. There was no answer to this. There was no way that this room could stay this way all these years. The people renting the house did not even know that the room existed because of the hidden door.

Tim, Tom, and Sallie began going through the papers. There was a ledger that showed where money was lent to different people in town. Each one was marked paid in full. Some had notes that said paid by a handshake, paid by a smile, or paid by a kindness to another person.

The only one that was not marked as paid in full was a man name Ted. They had no idea as to who Ted was, but at one point, he had borrowed twenty dollars, and it did not show as paid.

They continued going through the papers and furniture. There were many museum-worthy antiques in the room, and there were pictures of the town and its buildings from all through the years. The strangest thing was that the pictures continued to show progress for years long after their great grandfather had died. Some of the papers were as current as this year. How could this be? The room was locked. There were so many questions and so few answers.

Tim went back and looked at the book that showed Ted's name. He realized that the date was the same date that their great grandfather died. So there had been no way for Ted to repay his debt.

They continued looking through every box and book. The room was like a museum to the town of Rogerston. Every event that had been published in the paper about the town was there.

Sallie noticed a little opening which seemed to be yet another small door. They had flashlights and their phones. Was it safe? They did not know, but if one was going, all three were going.

As they opened up the door, they saw a round staircase that went down to the basement. At the bottom of the stairs was another door. This door led to a tunnel. The tunnel lead to a house next door. They went through the tunnel opening at that house and realized that they were now in the basement of someone's home. Perhaps this was the key to the things they had seen that day.

Suddenly a door opened. A tall thin man was standing in front of them. They had seen him in the diner but had never spoken. They were in his house.

He spoke to them and asked what they were looking for, and they began to tell him the story.

Ted's grandfather was a very young man when he found himself in debt. He went to the mayor and asked if he could borrow enough money to buy his wife and son some food to get them through to next payday. He was not only given that money, but every week for the next year, food was delivered to their house. The mayor had died, but they knew it was from him. So to make sure that the debt was always paid, Ted's grandfather, who had worked with the mayor to build the tunnel as an escape route in case of a town emergency, decided to make sure that the secret room would always be taken care of.

Ted's father had continued the tradition, and now he was continuing the tradition. He had never told anyone of this and not even his family knew of the hidden room.

This was a day that nobody had ever expected. They were surprised at every new discovery. Now the question was, what should be done about it? If the house was to be sold, then the things upstairs would be moved out.

Tom, Tim, and Sallie called and asked Ken and Jane to meet them at the mayor's office the next morning. They told them that the room that had been locked was full of things that the city may be interested in.

The next morning, they all met at the mayor's office. The three visitors told of what they had found, and Ted explained how he had come to be the keeper of the secret room.

As his father grew older and was not able to go up and down the stairs with ease, he had told Ted the story and had asked him to continue to do the work started by his grandfather. Ted had agreed. When Ted's parents passed away, he and his family moved into the house so that he could keep this secret and continue to take care of the room.

The people in the room decided that it was only right that the Stanley family be a part of the upcoming town picnic. They would take all the furniture, pictures, files, and ledgers to the town museum and keep it from the public until the weekend of the picnic. They would reveal the display which would be an exact replica of the room, right before the parade started. Tom, Tim, and Sallie would be the guests of honor and would be the parade masters of ceremony. As a part of their willingness to share their family's history with the town, they would be made honorary members of the town.

June was finally here. The weekend before the town picnic would be full of activities as things were being put into place. Everything was set and ready to go. As Friday approached, guests arrived in town. Loral Lake Inn was full, and the motel in town was almost totally booked. The biggest question that people seemed to be asking was, what was going on at the library?

The library had been closed for weeks, and the windows had been covered. A sign had been placed under the name of the library, but it was covered. What could the city council be up to? Why was the library closed, and why were the strangers from a few months ago back in town again?

Friday afternoon began with all of the floats lining up along the street in front of the library. The final decorations were completed, and the people were all ready to go. The town clock struck five, and the mayor began to speak. He welcomed everyone to the parade and to the weekend.

"I thank each of you for the hard work you have done in preparing for the parade. We are glad that everyone has come and are looking forward to a great weekend. Before the parade begins, I want to introduce you to three people that have certainly become a part of our community during the last few months.

Please welcome, Tom, Tim, and Sallie. They are the decedents of one of our town's former mayors, Mayor Stevens.

"Their grandparents, John and Ruth Stanley, lived here for many years in the house on the corner of Marion and Orr Streets. After the death of their grandmother, the house was rented to a family for nearly thirty years. Mr. Jones passed away last year, and Mrs. Jones has moved to the Loral Lake Retirement Center. Tom, Tim, and Sallie had come here to go through the house and fix it up to get it ready to sell.

"During their stay, they found some unexpected surprises that they have graciously donated to our town, which brings us to the work going on at the library. The parade will end at the library today at which time all information will be revealed. Please give a Rogerston welcome to our three masters of ceremony for the seventy-fifth town picnic parade, Tom, Tim, and Sallie."

Tom spoke for the family. "Thank each of you for the kindness shown to our family. As a special guest, we have asked Ted to also ride in the car with us. As you will soon learn, he has been a very important part of our history."

The parade began, and as said, it ended at the library which was at the end of the town. The crowd gathered around as the mayor began to speak and tell the story of all that had happened. The curtains to the library were pulled back, and the new sign was uncovered. The sign read, "The Home of the Mayor Stevens Memorial Room." People were allowed to walk inside and to be the first to view the new exhibit. It was spectacular, and as they all could see, the town's history was displayed from the years of Mayor Stevens until present day.

People left the library and headed to the lake for a night of music and dancing. At the dance, the towns' people had a chance to meet and talk to their special out-of-town guest and to hear more of the story.

During the dance, the mayor spoke and told the people that had not been at the beginning of the parade the story of Mayor Stevens. He gave each of them a chance to speak. Sallie spoke first and shared the memories she had as a young child and the visits to see her grandmother and, of course, the time at Loral Lake. Tim followed and explained how the family had come to make the decision to sell the house and start the repairs which lead to their discovery.

Finally Tom spoke. "I thank each of you for your kindness and the support you have shown our family. A very special thank-you to Ted for continuing his grandfather's work and keeping the 'secret room' as we found it. Ted, you will never know how much we appreciate you, and from our family to yours, we have marked your debt paid in full, with an extra big thank-you.

"For those of you who I have gotten to know over the last few months, I know that you have heard rumors that the house has already been sold. I want to let you know that it has and that the new owner will be moving in next week. It is with great honor that I tell you that I have decided to relocate to this great town. I knew that I wanted to move to a lake community when I retired. All of this happened to make that dream a reality. I have bought the house from Tim and Sallie, and with me living here, I know that all three of us will enjoy Rogerston and Loral Lake for many years to come. Now, on with the party."

The dance was over. Everyone went home, and the place was prepared for the next day. Booths were set up and ready. The vendors would arrive early, and the event would open at 10:00 a.m. The crowds continued to gather around the display that had been set up about the new library addition and asking questions. If nothing else came out of this new discovery in an old house, the town had something to talk about.

The day was a success, and the night was about to begin. Once again, the music would start, and the dancing would bring people to the floor. Mayor Smith spoke and encouraged everyone to stay and enjoy the night but to also make sure they joined us in the morning service the next morning.

After he finished, and the music started back, Tom walked over to Linda. "I finally figured it out," Tom started. "I knew that there was something that kept bringing me back to the diner, and last night as I went through another box of pictures, I finally knew why."

"What are you talking about? What did you figure out?" Linda asked.

"Oh, I think you already know the answer to this, don't you?

"Yes, I figured it out after you talked to Ken and Jane and told them where you were staying and why you were here," Linda agreed. "I did not want to mention it because I did not want you to feel uncomfortable because you did not remember me."

"I knew there was a reason that I felt so comfortable with you," Tom said. "That feeling of seeing an old friend just kept coming back. That is because you are an old friend. Oh, wait, not an old friend but a friend from a long time ago. You are the young girl that I wrote to all those years ago. But her name was not Linda. Her name was LM."

"Correct, LM is for Linda Marie," Linda explained. "When I went to high school, I was called by my first name in the classroom, so everyone started calling me Linda."

"Well then, Linda, will you dance with me?"

"I would be honored to, Tom."

At the end of the dance, Tom and Linda agreed to meet each other for the service the next morning. After all, the service was going to be at the lake, and what better place to spend a Sunday morning?

They joined Tim and Sallie, Ken and Jane, and the rest of the council for the picnic after the service. The picnic was the closing part of the weekend. They enjoyed the meal and reflected on all that had happened in such a short time. It was another successful and meaningful event that was held at Loral Lake—the perfect place.

About the Author

Nancy R. Ward was born in a small town in South Carolina where she has spent most of her life. She is a mother, grandmother, sister, friend, coworker, but most of all she is a child of God. She counts herself lucky to have the people in her life to share this adventure.

From an early age, she had a desire to write. During 2018, she decided that she was going to give writing a try and sat down at her computer. Within a few hours, her first short story was finished.

Being from a large family and having lived in the same area most of her life has provided her with many story lines and events to share. She has taken this and turned it into a collection of fictional short stories. It is her desire that these stories will add a smile to your face as you read.

She discovered that this was truly the outlet she had been looking for. She shared these stories with some of her family and coworkers. They encouraged her to send her stories to a publisher. And as the old saying goes, the rest is history.